WORMWOOD MIRE

ALSO BY JUDITH ROSSELL

Withering-by-Sea

WORMWOOD MIRE

Judith Rossell

A
atheneum

ATHENEUM BOOKS FOR YOUNG READERS
New York London Toronto Sydney New Delhi

ATHENEUM BOOKS FOR YOUNG READERS

An imprint of Simon & Schuster Children's Publishing Division

1230 Avenue of the Americas, New York, New York 10020

ATHENEUM BOOKS FOR YOUNG READERS is a registered trademark of Simon & Schuster, Inc. Atheneum logo is a trademark of Simon & Schuster, Inc.

For information about special discounts for bulk purchases, please contact Simon & Schuster Special Sales at 1-866-506-1949 or business@simonandschuster.com.

The Simon & Schuster Speakers Bureau can bring authors to your live event. For more information or to book an event, contact the Simon & Schuster Speakers Bureau at 1-866-248-3049 or visit our website at www.simonspeakers.com.

Book design by Debra Sfetsios-Conover

The text for this book was set in Adobe Jenson Pro.

The illustrations for this book were rendered in ink, pencil, watercolor, and digital work.

Manufactured in the United States of America

0617 FFG

First Edition

10 9 8 7 6 5 4 3 2 1

Library of Congress Cataloging-in-Publication Data

Names: Rossell, Judith, author, illustrator.

Title: Wormwood Mire / Judith Rossell.

Description: First edition. | New York : Atheneum Books for Young Readers, [2017] | Summary: The Aunts have sent eleven-year-old Stella away to the moldering old family estate, Wormwood Mire, where she discovers two odd cousins and more clues to the mysteries of her family and of herself.

Identifiers: LCCN 2016037884

ISBN 9781481443708 (hc)   ISBN 9781481443722 (eBook)

Subjects: | CYAC: Orphans—Fiction. | Aunts—Fiction. | Identity—Fiction. | Mystery and detective stories. | BISAC: JUVENILE FICTION / Family / Orphans & Foster Homes. | JUVENILE FICTION / Fantasy & Magic. | JUVENILE FICTION / Action & Adventure / General.

Classification: LCC PZ7.R719983 Wo 2017 | DDC [Fic]—dc23

LC record available at https://lccn.loc.gov/2016037884

For Henry, Isabel, Matthew, and Oscar

~๑ One ๑~

Stella Montgomery gazed out of the window of the train as it trundled slowly through the bleak countryside. It had been drizzling all day, and now evening was approaching. The empty compartment was cold and shadowy and dispiriting. In the lamp overhead, dregs of yellowish oil and several dead moths sloshed to and fro. Stella's new boots pinched her feet, and her new dress was stiff and uncomfortable. Pulling her coat more tightly around herself and burrowing her hands into the pockets, she stared out at the wintry trees.

She had never felt more lonely. She wished she had a friend for company. Even Ada, Aunt Deliverance's bad-tempered maid, would have been better than nobody. But after a grudging currant bun and a cup of tea at the station, Ada had pushed Stella into the second-class compartment, said, "Behave yourself, miss," and given her a silver shilling and a grumpy pat on the head. Then she had stalked away down the platform without looking back, and that was that.

Stella felt her eyes pricking with tears. She looked down at the little book that lay open on her lap. It had gold writing on its cover: *A Garden of Lilies: Improving Tales for Young Minds*, by Prudence A. Goodchild. The book had been a going-away present from the Aunts. It was full of depressing stories of children who did wrong and met with tragedy. In the first story, Agnes, a servant girl, wore vulgar, brightly colored ribbons in her hair and went to a fair, and so lost her position, became a beggar, and finally drowned in a river. The moral of that story was:

> *Modesty should be your aim,*
> *Or you will surely come to shame.*

In the next story, Beatrice stole a preserved damson, tried to wash the incriminating stains from her pinafore, and later died of a fever, brought on by the damp fabric.

> *Greedy children always tend*
> *To meet with a disastrous end.*

Cornelius and Drusilla disobeyed their parents and were trampled by a flock of angry sheep.

> *Always do as you are told,*
> *Or you will soon be dead and cold.*

It was not a cheerful book, and the pictures were vivid and rather unpleasant. Stella had read it all the way through three times. She sighed and tried to think of something encouraging, but she was too miserable and forlorn.

It had been a very long day. She had changed trains twice. The first change had occurred at an enormous, smoke-filled station, where she had been almost overwhelmed by the noise. A helpful porter had rushed her through the crowd at a desperate pace and bundled her into her train just as it was leaving. Despite this, she had somehow missed her second connection and had waited for several hours on a lonely country platform, with only the cold rain, a row of empty milk cans, and a station cat for company.

This train was the slowest so far. It wound its way

through the woods and fields and tiny huddled villages, sometimes stopping at stations where nobody seemed to get on or off, and sometimes stopping between stations for no reason at all.

The railway bun had been many hours ago, but Stella was too nervous to feel hungry. She blinked back her tears and swallowed. She did not want to arrive with her eyes red from crying. And if she started to cry, she might not be able to stop.

The Aunts had been furious. Stella had never seen them so angry. She had been in disgrace many, many times before. Even when she tried hard to be good, the Aunts were disapproving. But this time had been far worse. She had been missing for two nights. The police had been searching for her. And when she had returned, she had been dressed as a boy and covered with mud.

She had tried to explain how it had happened, but somehow it only made things worse. The Aunts refused to listen. Stella could almost hear Aunt Deliverance's bellowing voice, keeping time with the rattling train.

"Ungrateful. Willful. Obstinate. Unladylike."

"Disgraceful," Aunt Temperance had added, her wandering eye circling in an agitated manner.

"Yes, indeed," Aunt Condolence had agreed, her

Particular Patent Corset twanging and creaking.

All three Aunts glared at Stella, and she looked at her muddy boots and tried not to cry.

"I'm sorry," she muttered.

"Quiet!" Aunt Deliverance thundered. "Your behavior has been outrageous. We have been too indulgent with you entirely."

"Train the vine as you would have it grow," said Aunt Temperance.

"Spare the rod, spoil the child," said Aunt Condolence.

"A firm hand is required. Discipline. Perhaps a strict governess. Or school." Aunt Deliverance closed her mouth with a snap.

Stella's heart sank. A strict governess sounded terrifying. And school might be even worse. She had seen the girls of Miss Mallard's Academy for Young Ladies silently walking two by two along the Front at Withering-by-Sea. They seemed miserable, and their mistresses looked grim and bad-tempered. Any school chosen by the Aunts would be particularly dreadful.

For weeks she had been in disgrace. The weather had been terrible. Icy winds, rain, and storms had prevented the Aunts from taking their daily promenade along the Front. Instead they had stayed inside and glared at Stella as she walked around and around the parlor with a book balanced on her head (to improve her deportment), or sewed her sampler, or practiced the pianoforte.

Every day, Stella had learned difficult lessons from *French Conversation for Young Ladies* and repeated them to the Aunts as they had their tea. (*That parasol is quite hideous. Permit me to offer you a small piece of seed cake. These cold winds are injurious to the complexion.*)

Every day, she had cold porridge for breakfast, cold meat and potatoes for luncheon, and bread and water for supper.

Every day, she felt a bit more miserable.

At night she had leaned on the windowsill of her tiny bedroom on the third floor of the Hotel Majestic and looked out at the sea. Down along the pier, the gaslights twinkled in the rain. On still nights, she could hear the cheerful, tinkling music from the merry-go-round, and sometimes she imagined she could almost hear the band playing in the theater and the audience applauding. Her new friends were down there. Ben and Gert and Mr. Capelli. But they might as well be a hundred miles away. Her Aunts had forbidden Stella from seeing them again, and perhaps she never would.

Then, one morning, a letter had arrived with the first post. It was damp and salt-stained and looked as if it had been fished out of the sea. It had a row of colored foreign stamps on it. Aunt Deliverance opened the envelope with her ivory-and-silver paper knife, unfolded the letter, and read it through twice, in silence, as she ate her breakfast kipper. Then she had fixed Stella with an imperious glare.

"Cousin Frederick has at last listened to reason and sent his children home to be educated. And not before time."

Stella swallowed a mouthful of cold porridge too fast. "Who? But—"

"Quiet, child," Aunt Deliverance snapped. "I will not tolerate any of your imbecilic questions."

"Curiosity is a sign of a vulgar mind," said Aunt Temperance.

"Yes, indeed," agreed Aunt Condolence, spreading marmalade onto a triangle of buttered toast.

Aunt Deliverance continued, "It is extremely charitable of Cousin Frederick to allow you to join Strideforth and Hortense and their governess at Wormwood Mire."

Aunt Condolence made a choking sound, and Aunt Temperance started to say, "Not—"

Aunt Deliverance interrupted. "The house has an

unfortunate history, but it has been empty for ten years, without incident. Now that Frederick has inherited it, I imagine he wishes it to be occupied. I see no necessity for concern." To Stella, she said, "I trust you will be grateful and dutiful and obedient."

"Yes, Aunt Deliverance," Stella said, as gratefully and dutifully and obediently as she could manage. Frederick? She was astonished to learn that the Aunts had a cousin. They had never spoken of him.

"Frederick's children, Strideforth and Hortense, have been living abroad. No doubt their manners are foreign and disagreeable. However, a strict governess will correct any faults. They are being prepared for school. You will join them immediately." Aunt Deliverance glared as she popped a piece of kipper into her mouth and chewed it up in a decisive manner.

Stella had stared back at her and bitten her lip to stop the questions from spilling out.

She had always lived with the Aunts. First at the Ozone Hotel (where the Aunts had been treated with magnetism and leeches, which had sadly aggravated several of Aunt Deliverance's many illnesses), then at the Royal George Hotel (where the Aunts had taken cold-air baths and made use of the Influence Machine, which had caused Aunt Condolence's

Particular Patent Corset to hiss and spark in an alarming manner), then at the Hydro Imperial (where the Aunts had eaten a special diet of white food, consisting mainly of lard and tapioca and potato juice, which Aunt Temperance's insides had found intolerable), and finally at the Hotel Majestic, at Withering-by-Sea (where the Aunts drank the water, took wave baths, and walked briskly along the Front every day).

But now the Hotel Majestic was many miles behind her, and every minute Stella was moving farther away from the Aunts and closer to Wormwood Mire and the unknown cousins.

"Strideforth and Hortense," she whispered. They sounded dreadful. The Aunts were dreadful, of course, but at least they were familiar. The cousins would be strangers.

In another story from *A Garden of Lilies*, Euphemia went to stay in a castle. During dinner, she outraged the company by inadvertently using the wrong spoon to eat her giblet soup. Afterward she fell into an oubliette (whatever that was), and she was never seen again.

> *Boys and girls must all be able*
> *To eat correctly at the table.*

Stella imagined Strideforth and Hortense and their strict governess as tall, intimidating strangers, sitting at a long table that glittered with knives and forks and spoons and other more complicated cutlery. They all watched her coldly, waiting for her to make a mistake.

Her heart sank still further.

She knew nothing about her cousins, but she had heard of Wormwood Mire. She had seen pictures of it in Aunt Temperance's photograph album: an enormous dark house, bristling with towers and chimneys and turrets.

She turned the pages of *A Garden of Lilies* to find the stolen photograph she had tucked in there for safekeeping. She took it out and gazed at it. In the picture, part of a tall house, surrounded by trees, loomed against a cloudy sky. In front of the house, a young woman stood beside two babies in a perambulator. All three stared out of the photograph with startled eyes. Salt water had stained and blotched the picture. On the back was written, in faded sepia ink, *P, S & L, Wormwood Mire.*

Stella stared at the picture and chewed her lip. Her mother's name had been Patience. She had been the Aunts' youngest sister and died when Stella was still a baby. Was this a photograph of her? *P for Patience, S for Stella.*

But there were two babies. They looked identical, like twins. Who was *L*? Had she once had a sister? What had happened to her? The Aunts would never answer her questions. *Curiosity is vulgar, silence is golden*, Aunt Deliverance always said.

Stella looked at the two little faces in the photograph. She did not know much about babies. These looked about one or two years old. Perhaps someone at Wormwood Mire would remember a lady with two babies. Someone who had been there about ten years ago.

In the refreshment room at the railway station, Stella had tried to ask Ada about Wormwood Mire, and Ada had snapped, "That place should stay empty. It should be left alone to molder away."

Stella asked, "But—but why? What happened there?"

Ada did not look as if she would answer. Then she said abruptly, "Your Aunts were very good to take you in like they did. That I will say. Very good. Many wouldn't have, after what happened. If it was

11

me . . ." She stopped and looked at Stella, her lips tight and sour-looking, and she would say nothing more.

Stella looked out of the window of the train at the rain. She shivered as she remembered Ada's words. *After what happened.*

"I'm going to find out," she promised the three faces in the photograph. "I will." They stared back at her, wide-eyed.

Ever since she had found the photograph in Aunt Temperance's album, Stella had imagined a sister. Letty was the name she had chosen for her. She pictured her now, sitting here on the train, swinging her legs, cheerful and encouraging.

"What if it's awful?" she whispered.

Letty did not answer, but Stella imagined that she shrugged and laughed. Though Letty never said anything very much, she was a great comfort. She was always brave, and she made Stella feel braver too. Stella took one more look at the photograph, then put it carefully back between the pages of the book and slammed it shut. She sat up straighter and gazed out of the window.

The train was passing a wood. Trees grew closely together, like a crowd jostling for space. Their bare branches, tangled with ivy, created a jagged pattern against the sky. The raindrops running down the glass made the trees seem to flicker and tremble.

The wood looked wild and dark. Anything might live in the shadows.

Bears, perhaps. Or wolves.

In *A Garden of Lilies*, on their way to pay a morning call, Florence and Gilbert wandered from the correct path and were eaten up by a hungry tiger that had escaped from a circus.

> *Always go the way you should*
> *When you are walking through a wood.*

Of course there were no tigers here. There were no large, dangerous animals at all. Not anymore.

The train slowed, with grinding sounds and hissing steam, and drew into a station. It jolted to a stop.

"Wormwood Halt," called a porter.

Stella's insides gave a lurch. Heart thumping, she scrambled up onto the seat to pull her small suitcase down from the overhead rack. She opened it, shoved *A Garden of Lilies* inside, and snapped the catches shut. She pushed open the carriage door and climbed out.

"Wormwood Halt," called the porter again, in a

mournful tone, farther down the platform. "Alight here for Wormwood Halt."

It was nearly dark, and it was raining.

She had arrived.

❦ Two ❦

Stella made her way along the platform to the guard's van to collect her trunk. Her legs were stiff from sitting for so long. The train gave a loud whistle and began to move.

"Young lady for the Mire?" asked the porter as he heaved her trunk onto a trolley. He had a sack draped over his head and another around his shoulders, tied with twine. He smelled of onions.

"Yes. Wormwood Mire," said Stella, shivering.

"You're late," he said discouragingly. He led the way to the Ladies' Waiting Room and dumped her trunk down. "They came, but they went away again. They ordered the station coach. But the driver's gone for his dinner, and he ain't back yet. Put your case down here. You can wait in there." He pointed at the door.

The Ladies' Waiting Room was damp and cold and deserted. On the wall hung a clock, which had stopped, and an advertisement for Meat Extract. The fireplace was empty. There was a fly-spotted mirror and a washbasin. Stella looked into the mirror. Her hat was squashed, and her coat was grimy from the journey. There was a sooty mark on her cheek. She turned on the tap and a trickle of icy brown water came out. She rubbed at the soot with her damp handkerchief, spread it around a bit, and made it worse.

In another story from *A Garden of Lilies*, Horatio wore a grubby collar and immediately drowned in a shipwreck.

> *Be neat and tidy, clean and trim,*
> *Or your ending will be rather grim.*

Stella's eyes pricked with tears. *A Garden of Lilies* was not comforting at all. She missed her lovely Atlas. It had always been encouraging, even in the most difficult of circumstances. She sniffed, and a tear trickled down her cheek. Miserably, she gazed at herself in the mirror.

What would Letty do, if she were here? Certainly she would not just stand crying in this dismal waiting room.

Stella swallowed her tears and felt in her coat pocket for the shilling Ada had given her. She turned the little coin between her fingers. Perhaps she could buy some sweets? She could share them with the cousins, if they were friendly. And if they were not, she could eat the sweets herself.

"Come on, then," she said to her reflection.

She opened the door and looked out. The platform was empty. She walked past the booking office and across the station yard. A few people hurried along a narrow cobbled street, bundled up in coats and shawls. A sign with a picture of a huge black cat hung above the door of an inn: THE LEOPARD. Dim lights shone in the windows. Next to the inn was a stretch of muddy grass and a weedy pond. Several white ducks stood beside the pond in the rain. Beyond was a row of shops. Seen closer, they did not look promising. Several had already put up their shutters. She walked past a post office and a forge and a bakery. A grocer's window was full of dull jars and tins of tapioca and fish paste and isinglass, and an ironmonger's had a collection of nails and washboards.

Beyond the ironmonger, Stella spied a narrow, winding alleyway. At the far end, a greenish light shone from a curved bay window. The sign read:

Stella turned the small coin in her pocket, hesitating, and then she ventured into the alley. The upper stories of the buildings on either side nearly touched. Tendrils of ivy snaked along the walls, and the branches of a large tree arched overhead, making a dark tunnel.

Stella approached the little shop, cupped her hands, and peered through the rippled glass of the window. The shadowy interior swam with green light. It was like looking into a pond.

There was a row of sweet jars in the window. Treacle fudge, gleaming acid drops, cinder toffee, and aniseed balls. Barley sugar and striped black-and-white humbugs, shining like satin.

She climbed the two steps, pushed open the door, and went in. The bell above the door jangled. An oil lamp with a green glass shade hung from the ceiling. Shelves lined the walls, full of jars of sweets. There was a strong smell of peppermint and licorice, and something musty that she did not recognize.

Nobody came in answer to the bell.

"Good evening," Stella called. There was a scuffling sound. "Good evening?" she called again, her

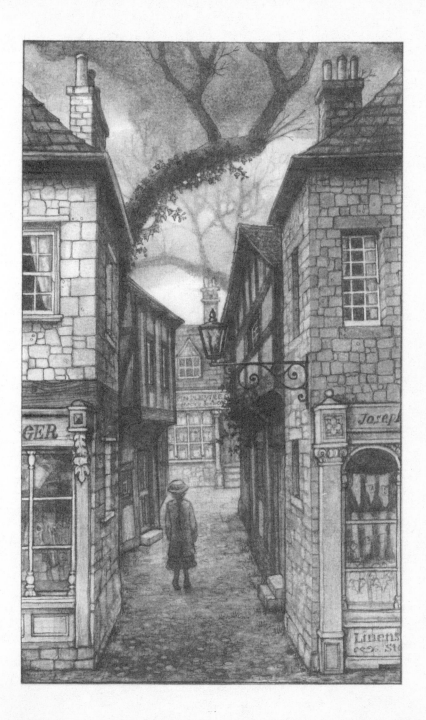

voice faltering. She thought she heard quick, pattering footsteps, but there was no reply.

She looked at the rows of sweets. A jar held a bundle of rough gray twigs tied with twine. She crouched to read the label: LICORICE ROOTS. The next jar was full of knobbly seedpods.

In the curved glass of the jar, a reflection moved. Stella turned around. Something shifted in a dark corner behind the counter.

"Is anyone there?" Her voice faltered a little more.

Her gaze fell on a jar that seemed to be full of cobwebs. Another contained dried leaves and several large snails. Their silver trails glinted in the greenish light.

Perhaps this was not such a good idea after all. She took a step toward the door.

Suddenly a flurry of raindrops struck the window and a pale shape swooped past outside. A shutter banged, an owl hooted, and something scrabbled on the floor of the room above. There was a cough, and then heavy footsteps dragged across the floor and started down the stairs. A hoarse voice called, "Who's there? Tick? Is that you?"

Stella clutched her hands together.

An old woman shuffled behind the counter. She had white hair and a hooked nose, and was wrapped in a black shawl, embroidered with a pattern of feathers and stars. She started to say something, but then she shot out a hand, wrinkled like the claw of a bird, and clasped Stella's wrist. "Who are you? Who?" Her voice was fierce. Her wide eyes were a strange light yellow.

"I—I—" Stella stammered. Panic rising, she tried to pull away. "I'm sorry, I have to go." She wrenched her arm free and darted to the door. Her fingers scrabbled on the handle. She flung the door open, setting the bell jangling again, half fell down the stairs, and fled back along the narrow alley.

Stella's feet skidded on the muddy ground as she raced out of the alley and into the street. Gasping for air, she looked over her shoulder, but there was nothing to see. She hugged her arms around herself as she hurried back along the street, weaving between people, past the shops and the inn.

In the station yard, an old-fashioned coach was waiting. The coachman was helping the porter to load Stella's trunk and suitcase. As she came toward them, Stella heard him say, "Three sheep gone, Tom Pintucket says. It's back, surely. It will be a child next, mark my words."

"Fiddle-faddle," said the porter. "Nonsense. It ain't been seen for ten years, or thereabouts. It's long dead."

"Cobbin' great thing, Tom says. Teeth like—" The coachman saw Stella and stopped.

The porter turned. "There you are, miss. Where'd you get to? Here's the fly."

"Thank you," said Stella, her heart hammering.

"It's near on dark," said the coachman with a quick look over his shoulder.

The porter said, "Best get going, then," and gave one of the horses a slap.

The coachman said something as he helped Stella up, but the sound of rain on the roof drowned his words.

"Thank you," she said as he slammed the door.

The interior of the coach smelled of damp straw. Stella groped around, felt the cracked leather seat, and clambered up.

Outside, the coachman spoke in a hurried, anxious voice and the porter grunted a reply. Then the coachman climbed up and growled to the horses, and the coach jolted and trundled out of the station yard.

A few people were hurrying through the rain. In

one of the cottages, someone looked out from a window before slamming the shutters.

Beyond the village, the road wound between fields of dejected-looking shaggy sheep and rocks and brambles and clumps of trees. Farmhouses were dark, huddled shapes in the dusk. Stella realized she was clutching her hands together so tightly her fingers hurt. She felt as if a large, cold frog were leaping around her insides. She took a breath and pushed her hands into the pockets of her coat.

The coach bumped along the winding lanes, its lights flickering on the overgrown hedgerows. Presently it stopped with such a jerk that Stella was almost flung from her seat. She peered out of the window to see a high stone wall. Along the top was a row of rusty spikes. A pair of curly iron gates was set in a tall archway. A light shone from the window of a small gatehouse. The coachman blew his horn, and after a moment a hunched figure stumped out, unlocked the gates, and heaved them open.

The coach passed through the archway. The road sloped downward into an overgrown garden; it was like plunging into dark water. The coachman cracked his whip to hurry the horses along. The coach bounced and plunged and swayed, and Stella clung on, heart thumping. Mist drifted amongst the trees.

Palms and ferns with large, spiky leaves loomed in the flickering coach lights.

The coach slowed and jolted to a stop at the front of an enormous house.

Stella unlatched the door and clambered down into the rain.

The coachman unloaded the luggage and carried it up the curving steps to the door. He dumped it down in the shelter of the portico.

Stella said, "Wait, please—" as he turned to go.

"Ring the bell, miss," he grunted, and with a nervous look over his shoulder, he added, almost reluctantly, "Mind you stay inside after dark." Then he hurried back to the coach, climbed up, and drove away quickly, cracking his whip.

Stella watched the coach until it was out of sight and the glimmer of its lights was lost amongst the trees. She was shaking, partly from cold and partly from fright. She spied the iron bellpull beside the door. She took a breath, grasped it, and pulled it down.

⋘ Three ⋙

There was a coughing wheeze, a long pause, and then a crashing, clattering sound echoed from somewhere far inside the dark house, as if a load of saucepans were being banged together.

Stella looked up. Towers and chimneys and carved stone animals loomed above her. Raindrops pattered down. In the overgrown garden, trees tangled with vines made uncanny, shadowy shapes.

A night creature gave a drawn-out, mournful cry. Something took flight with a sound like an umbrella being shaken. There was a crash of branches.

Stella imagined Letty was standing beside her. "What was that?"

Before Letty could answer, a harsh scream from inside the house made Stella jump. She took two steps away from the door, her heart beating in her throat. The scream came again, louder and closer.

Stella felt herself begin to fade, as she sometimes did when she was trying to hide. Like a wisp of smoke dissolving into the air. She took a deep breath and forced the horrible, dizzying feeling away. She did not want to disappear. What would the cousins say, if they knew she was so strange? That she was fey? What would they think of her? She hoped they would never find out.

She gripped her hands together tightly, feeling the bones in her fingers, solid and reassuring.

The bolts were drawn back with a squeal, and the door opened with a reluctant grinding of hinges.

A light glimmered.

A large white bird flapped out.

Stella shrieked. She put her hands up to shield her eyes and felt the beating of wings.

A little girl darted out, waving her arms. The bird gave a scream and flew away into the rainy dark.

"Did he frighten you? I'm sorry. He wouldn't hurt you. Not really."

Stella turned to see a boy of about her own age. He was stocky, with untidy black hair and dark eyes.

"That was Henry. He's a mollymawk." The boy was bundled up in a hairy coat, so he looked rather like a small, shaggy bear. A long scarf was wound around his neck, and he was carrying a lantern. He pushed the last bit of a jam sandwich into his mouth and shook Stella's hand. "How do you do?" he said with his mouth full. "I'm Strideforth. This is my sister, Hortense." He spoke quickly, with a slight foreign accent.

The girl was two or three years younger than the boy. She was wrapped in an embroidered velvet curtain that trailed on the ground behind her. She had tangled dark hair, the same dark eyes as her brother, and a solemn expression. She put out her hand.

"I'm Stella," said Stella as she shook hands.

Strideforth said, "We're very pleased to see you. We met your train, but you weren't on it. We thought you weren't coming after all. Did you hear the bell? The wire was rusted and broken. I fixed it. And I improved it too. It's very loud now."

Hortense cupped her hands around her mouth and made a harsh cry. The bird flew down out of the dark and landed heavily on her head, making her stagger. He looked like a large seagull. His front was gleaming white and his back was gray. A black line on his brow made him appear to be frowning. He clicked his beak several times and cackled at Stella. Then he unfolded his long wings and flew back into the house.

"Hortense rescued Henry when he was a chick," said Strideforth. "He thinks she is his mother. He's very bad." Hortense scowled at Strideforth, and he said, "Oh, he is, Hortense. He is very, very bad. He steals things and tears them to bits." He passed her the lantern, grabbed Stella's trunk by the handle, and heaved it over the threshold. He closed the door and bolted it. He said, "I'll ask Mr. Burdock to help take your trunk up later. Can I carry your case now?"

"Thank you." Stella passed him the suitcase and looked around the hallway. Magnificent stairs curved up into darkness. Wallpaper with a complicated curly pattern of gold vines gleamed in the lantern light. The head of a large animal with long, pointed horns gazed down with a glassy expression. Cobwebs and dust covered everything.

"This way," said Strideforth. He led them through a carved archway and along a wide passage. The wallpaper here hung in damp, curling strips. Henry flew ahead, his loud cries echoing.

"Dining room. Moroccan drawing room," said Strideforth, pointing at doors. "Music room. Chinese parlor. Come on. Are you cold? It's warm in the kitchen."

They went through a doorway, along another passage, past rows of paintings and glass cases containing a scattering of moldering insects and broken sea-shells. A stuffed bird with dusty black feathers and a hooked beak stared at them, its eyes glinting.

"Wilberforce Montgomery built this house"—Strideforth turned around and walked backward—"a long time ago. He was our ancestor, you know. Our great-great-grandfather. And yours, too, I think. He was a collector. And he brought things back here from everywhere. Animals and bones and birds' eggs. All kinds of things. He was famous for it. Look, there's a picture of him." He pointed to a large portrait in an ornate frame. "There. That's him."

Stella looked at the painting with interest. She had never had an ancestor before. Wilberforce Montgomery was a plump, cheerful-looking man wearing an old-fashioned white wig. He sat in a summerhouse in a garden, beside a lake, surrounded by plants and birds, a pile of books, and a globe of the world.

Below the picture, a large, rusty iron pipe snaked along the wall. Strideforth bent down and felt it. "This is quite cold," he said. He tapped the pipe with his finger, then put his ear to it and frowned.

"Do you live here all by yourselves?" asked Stella as they went up a narrow, winding staircase, their shadows looming and flickering.

Strideforth said, "There's Miss Araminter, of course. She is our governess. And Mr. Burdock and Mrs. Burdock. And Jem, their grandson. They are the caretakers. Mrs. Burdock takes our washing. And Mr. Burdock looks after the furnace. They live up in the gatehouse. And the postman comes sometimes."

"Aren't there any servants?"

"No. The people in the village don't like coming here. They believe in all kinds of things. Ghosts and monsters. They won't go outside after dark. But that is all nonsense. There are no such things. That is certain. It is unscientific."

Strideforth sounded very sure. But Stella knew

there were sometimes unexplained things in the world, little trickles of magic. She remembered how reluctant the coachman had been to drive out here and how quickly he had hurried away, and she shivered. She said, "It's a big house."

"Yes. Forty-six rooms," said Strideforth. "I counted them. And perhaps more in the main tower. We couldn't find the way up there."

"I heard something," Stella said. "Big and flapping. In the garden."

"Probably a peacock," said Strideforth. "They're huge. And they make a dreadful noise. You do it, Hortense."

Hortense made a loud, mournful cry.

"Was that it?" asked Strideforth.

Stella nodded.

Strideforth said, "And there are huge big bats living in one of the attics, too, perhaps from Java, Miss Araminter thinks. We found a parrots' nest in the library. And Mrs. Burdock says last year a fox had cubs in the Turkish smoking room." They had reached a narrow, winding passageway lined with doors. "We're living right at the back here in the servants' wing, above the kitchen. These used to be the servants' bedrooms along here. They're empty now, of course. This is Miss Araminter's room, this one's mine, and this one's for Hortense and you." He pushed open a door.

The small room contained two beds. They were covered with blankets and velvet curtains, like the one Hortense was wrapped in. In the lantern light, they gleamed with gold thread.

Strideforth laid Stella's suitcase on the bed closest to the window and crouched down to feel an iron pipe that curled along the wall. "Be careful, these pipes get hot. At least, they are supposed to. There's a furnace in the cellar."

Stella took off her coat and hat and pulled off her gloves. She rubbed her cold fingers together and looked around the room. It seemed to have been furnished with odd bits and pieces, but it was cozy and welcoming. It had a small window, a plain wardrobe, and a fancy gilt dressing table with a large mirror. The rug had been cut from a much bigger carpet. The pattern was a small piece of an enormous rose that must have originally been the size of a wagon wheel.

"I hope you don't mind sharing with Hortense," said Strideforth.

Stella had never shared a bedroom before, but she did not want to be alone here, in this huge, empty house. She said, "Of course not."

Hortense did not say anything.

Stella wondered if the little girl could speak at all. As if in answer, Strideforth said, "Hortense prefers animals to people. She used to talk, but not so much anymore. Not since Mother died. Mrs. Burdock says she's willful and stubborn, but Miss Araminter just says she will talk when she is ready."

Hortense frowned, and Stella was startled to see a tiny pointed face peeping out from her tangled dark hair. The little creature had a long body like a weasel, white fur, and bright eyes like jet beads. Stella reached out with her finger, but it chittered angrily and snapped at her. Stella jumped back. Hortense chirruped at it, but it darted behind her neck and was gone.

Strideforth said, "That's Anya. She's an ermine. Hortense got her from a Russian sailor on the ship. She's little, but she's very fierce. You have to watch her because she bites everyone."

Hortense scowled at him.

Strideforth said, "Oh, you know she does, Hortense. She bites everyone. She bit all the sailors, and the passengers, and the captain, and the ticket collector on the train, and even that lady who was

33

just standing there at the station and also her dog, and Miss Araminter, and Mr. Burdock, and Mrs. Burdock. And Jem. And the postman. And me. She bites everyone. There is nobody she does not bite, except you. That sailor was very, very happy to give her away." He grinned. "Are you ready, Stella? You must be hungry and cold. It's much warmer in the kitchen."

᭥᭥᭥ *Four* ᭥᭥᭥

Strideforth led the way down the narrow staircase. "The privy is out here, if you need it," he said, pointing along a dark passageway. "I improved it. I took it apart to see exactly how it works, and then I put it back together. It's much better now. More efficient. And more interesting. Come on, I'll show you."

The privy was very cold. Water dripped down the mossy brick walls. This was quite different from the Hotel Majestic, where the plumbing was extremely modern and sparkling crystals hung from the gaslights. Stella used the lavatory quickly.

From the other side of the door, Strideforth called, "Pull the chain hard."

Stella felt for the chain in the darkness and gave it a tug.

"Both hands," called Strideforth. "Put your whole weight on it."

She grabbed the chain and yanked it down. There was a clunking sound, a loud metallic thumping, and then a surging rush of splashing, icy water. When she emerged, dripping, Strideforth grinned proudly and said, "See? Come on. The kitchen's along here."

They went along a series of winding, flagstone passageways. "Shoe room, knife room, butler's pantry," said Strideforth. "Here's the furnace."

A flight of stone steps led down to a cavernous cellar, full of clanking and banging and hissing steam. The furnace filled the room. It was the size of a small whale and bristled with complicated-looking dials and levers. Iron pipes snaked off in all directions, like the tentacles of a monstrous metal octopus. Strideforth rubbed a bit of shiny brass with the sleeve of his coat.

"An engineer came to clean it and make it work again. Mr. Burdock looks after it, and I help him. It burns coal that comes down that chute there, from the yard," he said, pointing. "The pipes lead everywhere, all through the house. I haven't traced them all yet. I've been making some diagrams. It's very interesting." He waved his arm at some scratchy drawings pinned to the wall. "When it's working properly,

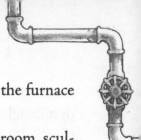

the whole house will be warm." He gave the furnace a pat and grinned proudly once more.

They climbed back up the stairs. "Stillroom, scullery, larder," said Strideforth. "Here's the kitchen." It was at the end of the passageway, a long room with an arched ceiling. A huge range filled one wall. A fire glowed in the grate. Iron pipes curled up the walls and across the ceiling, groaning and hissing.

Henry was walking sideways along the mantelpiece, jabbing things with his beak and muttering. He screamed cheerfully when he saw them and flapped his wings. Hortense screamed back at him.

"Sit here, Stella, near the range," said Strideforth.

She sat down and looked around. High up on one wall was a row of servants' bells: BALLROOM, JAPANESE DRAWING ROOM, YELLOW BEDROOM. Drawings of birds and plants and animals were pinned on the walls. A mixed group of wooden kitchen chairs and gilt armchairs stood around a large table, which was covered with all kinds of things: books, empty tins, pens and ink, an arrangement of preserved ferns in a glass dome, a row of tiny plants growing in teacups, a magnifying glass, some kind of chemical apparatus, and a sewing basket. A cupboard was stacked with plates and cups and pots and pans.

"That's the doorbell there," said Strideforth,

pointing up to a collection of tea trays and old tins that dangled from a wire, connected to several pulleys and a knotted rope that disappeared into the ceiling. "You were the first visitor since I fixed it. It worked well. It was very, very loud. We all jumped." He took off his coat and unwound his scarf. "Can you cook?" he asked.

"No," said Stella.

"We can't either. We hoped you might be able to. We mostly eat bread and cheese from the village. And we found lots of old jam in the larder. Blackberry, we think." He waved at a jar of dark jam on the table. "And Mrs. Burdock brings us apples and walnuts, and sometimes eggs, when she is not cross with us, which she generally is, and once she made us a rabbit stew. That was very good. And Father sent us a hamper." He rummaged in a large wicker basket packed with straw. "So we had lots of different things in tins: curried chicken, pineapple, biscuits, sardines and mackerel for Henry. We've nearly finished them, but we've been saving this last one for when you came." He held up a tin with a colorful label. "It's a plum pudding. It looks good." He dropped the tin gingerly into a saucepan of boiling water on the range.

Something moved on the floor beside Stella's foot.

She looked down. A little hedgehog was sniffing around the leg of her chair.

"That's Teasel," said Strideforth. "Hortense found her in the garden. She likes snails. And she eats all the cockroaches and black beetles in the 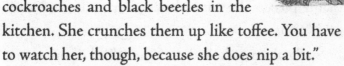 kitchen. She crunches them up like toffee. You have to watch her, though, because she does nip a bit."

Hortense made a grunting sound, and the hedgehog answered her. The little creature looked up at Stella with bright, beady eyes before wandering away under the table.

"Look at this," said Strideforth. He picked up a loaf of bread and pushed it inside a contraption that was made from pieces of metal, bits of wire, cogs, and wheels. He turned a handle on the top. "Watch out," he said. Stella looked around nervously. Hortense covered her head with her hands. Henry gave a shriek. There was a clanking sound, a whir, and several torn-off pieces of bread shot out of the contraption and spun across the room.

"It's a bread-slicing machine," Strideforth said proudly as he collected the scattered, raggedy pieces of bread from distant corners of the kitchen. "It's a very good invention. More interesting than a knife. I built it from a bread box and the insides of a clock.

It's no use with cheese, though. It just smashes it to pieces." As he was talking, he cut slices of cheese with his pocketknife and quickly made a pile of lopsided sandwiches. He passed one each to Stella and Hortense. He gave a piece of cheese to Henry on the mantelpiece. The bird shrieked happily, and then said, "*Gratias.*"

Stella almost choked on a mouthful of bread and cheese. "He talks?"

"It's Latin. I have to learn Latin for school." Strideforth pulled a face. "But it is very useless, I think. And not interesting at all. Henry thinks he knows more than me. But he does not. He is just showing off." He frowned at Henry, who cackled and fluffed up his feathers. "I like to find out how things work. Miss Araminter is teaching me mathematics and engineering and drawing. And Hortense is learning drawing too, and zoology, which she likes. And French and mathematics, which she does not like so much. And botany. That's why Father sent us home. For our education. Father says it's time we were more proper and correct. He wants me to learn Latin and Greek, and Hortense to learn how to play the pianoforte and dance, and talk to people and not so much to animals, he says."

"Where were you before?" asked Stella.

"Tribulation Island." Strideforth sat down on a chair beside her, took a big bite of his sandwich, and spoke with his mouth full. "Father's a lighthouse keeper."

"Oh," Stella breathed. She wished she could look it up in her Atlas. "What is it like?" she asked.

"Very cold and windy, and snow and ice in the winter. Lots of seals and penguins. The lighthouse is very interesting. The lamp burns whale oil and rotates by clockwork. It must be wound up every two hours, all night. I helped to look after it." Strideforth paused. Then he said, "Every month a ship comes with supplies. Flour and tea and sugar and oil and letters and hampers. Father loves hampers. He loves food in tins."

Hortense sniffed and stroked Anya.

Strideforth went on sadly, "But this time he sent us away on the ship. He always said that he would send us away to school, when we were old enough. He promised Mother, before she died. We thought perhaps it would not be until next year, or the year after that. Or perhaps never. But then something unfortunate happened. I improved his bed. With clockwork. To help him wake up early in the morning. You wind it up"—Strideforth demonstrated, waving his sandwich in a circle—"and set the time.

41

There's a pivot. And a spring. And in the morning, the whole bed spins over and dumps you very hard on the floor. It was a good invention, and much better than an alarm clock, and more interesting, too. But Father was not so happy. It is not proper and correct to dump your father on the floor like that. And then Hortense invited many penguins into the lighthouse for a party and gave them sardines from tins and tea and biscuits. Which they liked a lot, but Father did not like at all. They made a lot of noise and mess, and they broke many teacups and also the lid of the sugar bowl. And then Henry tore up a book of lighthouse regulations and signals into tiny pieces. And then Father shouted a lot, and said enough is enough, and now we are old enough to go away, first to have a governess and then to go to school."

Strideforth sighed. "Father hated school. He said it was dreadful. Very, very cold and there is horrible food. Porridge with big lumps in it, and boiled white-fish that tastes like washing, and a kind of pudding that is like frog spawn, but with skin on top. And other things even more terrible than that. Father ran away from school many times. At last he hid on a ship that went all the way to the Argentine, where he met Mother. But when Mother died, Father was very unhappy, and so were we. And then we went to live on

Tribulation Island." Strideforth shrugged. "And now we will go to school. Gloamings for me—that is the same school that Father went to—and Wakestone Hall for Hortense. He has written to them, and we will start next term. It will be very, very dreadful, that is certain."

Stella wondered what would happen to her when the cousins went to school. Would she go too? She asked, "What is your governess like? Is she very strict?"

"Father advertised for a governess in the *Times*. Miss Araminter was the only one who would come here. None of the others would, because the house is empty and there are no servants, and it is so far from everywhere. She is nice, but she is only interested in—" He broke off as Henry gave an earsplitting cry and flapped up into the air. At the far end of the room, a door opened and a tall woman strode into the kitchen in a purposeful manner. She was wet through. She wore a long cape and an extraordinary hat decorated with twigs and leaves. She carried an enormous black umbrella, a lantern, and an armful of dripping plants.

She said, "Stinking gladwyn, Siberian thistle, devil's-bit, Tibetan fogwort, I believe. And a marvelous Batavian buttercup."

Henry landed on her hat with an affectionate scream. "*Heus!*" he shrieked.

"Here's Stella," said Strideforth, waving his arm. "Stella Montgomery, Miss Araminter. Our governess."

"My dear. You have arrived at last. How do you do?" Miss Araminter passed the umbrella and the lantern to Strideforth and the bundle of plants to Hortense. She shooed Henry off her head, swooped down, and shook Stella's hand with both of hers. She had an interesting face, bony and expressive. She smiled. "Welcome to Wormwood Mire," she said. "We are so very pleased to have you with us."

✺✹ *Five* ✹✺

M iss Araminter pulled off her gloves and
rubbed her hands together. She took off
her wet hat and cape and hung them up. "Charming
evening for a brisk walk in the garden," she said as
she took the bundle of wet plants from Hortense.
Strideforth passed her a cheese sandwich on a plate.
"Thank you, my dear," she said, and sat down at the
table. She ate in an inattentive manner as she gazed at
Stella. "Did you have a pleasant journey?" she asked.

"Yes, thank you, Miss Araminter."

The governess poked her long fingers into the pile
of plants. "Are you interested in botany at all?"

"I don't know," said Stella doubtfully.

"There are some fascinating plants in the garden. Wilberforce Montgomery was a famous collector. He built this house and garden to hold his

collection. It was rather modern, for its time. Splendid heating system, all these pipes everywhere. And he drained the mire, built the lake, and brought back many plants and animals and other curiosities from foreign places. The museum took most of his collection, and of course the animals went to the zoo. But the plants are still here. I am exploring the garden and finding many interesting specimens. There is a quite enormous monkey puzzle on the front lawn and a delightful Chinese pagoda tree down near the lake. The leaves are an emetic." She noticed Stella's puzzled face. "They induce vomiting," she explained.

Stella wondered why anyone would want to induce vomiting, but she did not like to ask.

"And there is a wonderful colony of dragon orchids on the hillside behind the stables. Extremely rare and rather lethal, my dear, so do be careful. And who knows what other treasures lurk in the shrubberies? Many surprising things thrive here, as the valley is very sheltered. I have encountered some marvelous foreign slugs. And yesterday I came across a huge centipede, perhaps from Brazil. Are you interested at all in large, poisonous invertebrates, my dear?"

Startled, Stella shook her head.

"Are you sure? There may be a book in the library," said Miss Araminter. She extracted a plant from the pile and sniffed it, her long, bony nose quivering.

"Now, this is devil's-bit. A charming herb. Would you be so kind as to consult Culpeper?"

Stella looked where the governess was pointing and pulled a leather-bound book from under a heavy green stone on a nearby chair.

Culpeper's Complete Herbal
By Nich. Culpeper, Gent.
Student in Phyfick and Aftrology

She laid it on her lap and leafed through the pages. The paper was thin and crinkly, like the skin of an onion. The words were difficult to read, the printing dense and black, and some of the letters were unfamiliar shapes, stretched out long and thin or jammed up together. There were pictures of different plants, beautifully colored.

Bazil. Betony. Bishop's Weed. Stella turned the pages. *Daifies. Dandelion. Darnel. Devil's-Bit.* She tilted the book to the lantern light and carefully followed the words with her finger as she read out, "'The diftilled water of the herb is very effectual for green wounds and old sores . . .'"

Henry edged sideways along the mantelpiece and made a sudden flapping pounce on the book.

Stella gasped, snatched it away, and clutched it to her chest. Hortense made some loud squawking sounds to him, and he backed away with an angry cluck, his head cocked.

"You have to watch him around books and paper, my dear," said Miss Araminter. "He does enjoy tearing things up. And he will steal things. He is rather unprincipled."

Stella noticed that all the books in the room were held down by heavy objects: a glossy purple crystal, a fossil, a stone rabbit.

Keeping a cautious eye on Henry, she opened the book again and continued reading: "'. . . sores, scurf, itch, pimples, freckles, morphew, or other deformities . . .'"

"Morphew. Marvelous. Thank you, my dear. I will make a distillation," said Miss Araminter, tasting a leaf of the devil's-bit. "Mr. Burdock has such trouble with his feet. Perhaps this will help." She pushed her plate aside, dipped a pen into an ink bottle, and made some quick, pecking notes in a journal.

"Miss Araminter is writing a book," said Strideforth, biting into another sandwich. "*Some Reflections on the*

Properties of Plants, by A Lady. Fully Illustrated." He pointed to a thick pile of pages held down by a large marble foot, part of a broken statue.

"Tomorrow we will begin your studies, my dear," said Miss Araminter as she connected a glass tube to a rubber hose. "Botany? Essential. The queen of the sciences. We can learn everything we need to know about the world from the study of plants. Observation and experimentation, that's the key, I believe. And perhaps also Latin with Strideforth? Zoology, mathematics, and engineering? And drawing?"

"I've never learned them," said Stella uncertainly. Lessons had always been deportment and French with Aunt Temperance, and needlework and pianoforte with Aunt Condolence. All equally disagreeable.

"Then there is no time to lose," Miss Araminter said. "You and Strideforth are of an age. You will be able to study together."

Strideforth was attacking the hot plum-pudding tin with his pocketknife. He grinned at Stella as he levered the top off the tin with a screwdriver-like attachment and began scooping the steaming contents out into a bowl.

She said, "I'll try."

Miss Araminter flashed her a sudden smile. "We have lessons in the morning, dinner at midday, and you will have preparation to complete in the afternoon. And no doubt you have your own studies to pursue. The library here is old-fashioned and rather damp, but you may find something of interest."

"Can—I mean, may I read the books?" asked Stella, stroking the cover of *Culpeper's Complete Herbal*. With the Aunts, her only books had been the dull *French Conversation for Young Ladies*, the depressing *A Garden of Lilies*, and her beloved Atlas. She had kept the Atlas hidden because if her Aunts had ever found it, they would have had it burned. She had given it away, and she missed it enormously.

Strideforth passed her a bowl of plum pudding. It was hot, and smelled of cloves and cinnamon and raisins and treacle.

"Of course," said Miss Araminter. "You must read anything you like, my dear."

Stella smiled for what felt like the first time in weeks.

❧

Later, in her bedroom, Stella prepared for bed, listening to the huge house creaking and settling. From somewhere far below came echoing, sighing sounds and trickling water. Hortense was already asleep, her arm flung around Henry. He was snoring, his head tucked under his wing. Anya was a tiny white ball tangled in Hortense's dark hair, and Teasel was a little pincushion on her pillow.

It was odd to think she had been here before, when she was a baby.

"What will it be like living here?" she whispered to Letty.

She imagined that Letty giggled, which was somewhat encouraging.

It felt strange to have no maid to help her undress and fold her clothes, but Stella did the best she could. She found her nightgown and pulled it on over her head.

She washed her face in icy water and brushed her hair. It didn't hurt as much as when Ada did it, yanking the brush through the knots and scolding all the time. In *A Garden of Lilies*, Isadora did not brush her hair properly, and straightaway fell from the top of a high cliff into the ocean and was swallowed by a large fish.

> *For hair that's glossy, clean and bright,*
> *Two hundred strokes, both morn and night.*

Sighing, Stella struggled with the tangles in her hair, plaited it with some difficulty, and tied the end with a piece of ribbon.

The large mirror above the dressing table was flyspecked, and parts of the silvery backing had come away. The uneven surface of the mirror made her reflection shift and change. For a moment, Stella did not recognize herself. It seemed as if she were looking into the pale face of a stranger, but someone who looked just like her. She gave herself a tentative smile, and her reflection smiled back uncertainly.

She shivered and crawled into bed. The sheets felt damp. The pillow was lumpy and uncomfortable. She was very sleepy. An owl hooted in the garden. Stella blew out the candle, pulled the blankets over her head, and fell asleep.

Stella dreamed she was walking through a dense wood, singing to herself under her breath. Overhead, the twisting branches stretched up into the night sky. Raindrops pattered down all around. Somewhere in the darkness, she heard a fox yelp and a nightjar's churring call. Above, a pale shape swooped. An owl, hunting. She froze, fading into the shadow, until the owl passed by, and then she crept on, her feet silent on the wet leaves.

❧

When Stella woke up the next morning, the room was cold. In the grayish early morning light, it looked shabbier and less mysterious than it had the night before. Hortense's bedclothes had been flung onto the floor, and her bed was empty.

Stella climbed out of bed, tiptoed to the window, and opened the curtains. It was misty and raining. She unlatched the window and pushed it open. Some little birds fluttered about, twittering, but when they saw her, they darted away. Below the window was an overgrown kitchen garden, tangled with brambles and nettles.

A loud squawk came from somewhere above. She poked her head out and looked upward. Henry was perched on top of one of the stone pineapples that decorated the edge of the roof. He frowned at her, then spread his long wings, swooped down, and landed with a thump on the windowsill. Stella stepped back nervously. In daylight, she could see he was a handsome bird. His feathers were glossy and beaded with raindrops. But he was rather large, and his beak looked strong and sharp. She took another step away from him. He flapped in through the window and landed on the dressing table, knocking her hairbrush and comb onto the floor.

"*Salve*," he said sternly.

"Um," said Stella. "Good morning."

He eyed the tumbled clothes in her open suitcase. He hopped down and jabbed at them with his beak. He tugged her bath bag out by its string and flung it onto the floor. He poked at her underclothes, muttering to himself, then dived into the suitcase and dragged out *A Garden of Lilies*, pages flapping.

"No, no," said Stella hastily. "Please don't." She tried to snatch the book from him, but he evaded her and pulled it under her bed, cackling. Stella lay down on the floor and peered at him. He was holding the book down with a huge webbed foot and tearing it apart. "No!" she said, as firmly as she could manage. "No. Please stop."

Henry ripped the spine off the book with enthusiasm.

Someone knocked on the door. "Stella? Are you awake?"

"Come in," she said, scrambling to her feet.

Strideforth opened the door and entered the room. He was eating a ragged piece of bread and jam. Hortense followed him, carrying a cup. Anya, the ermine, was perched on her shoulder. Hortense placed the cup carefully on the mantelpiece.

"Good morning," said Strideforth. "Did you sleep well? We brought you some cocoa. Your trunk's outside here." He put his hand on the iron pipe. "It's cold again. I don't know what's wrong with it. The heat must be going somewhere. It's very interesting—" He broke off, hearing the busy tearing sounds from under the bed. "What's happening?"

"Henry's got my book."

Strideforth pushed the bread and jam into his pocket, threw himself down, and crawled under the bed. "No, Henry!" he said. "Give it to me." There were sounds of a struggle, angry shrieking, more tearing, and then Strideforth came out backward, clutching the remains of *A Garden of Lilies* to his chest. Bits of paper fluttered everywhere. He had a scratch on his cheek.

"I'm sorry." He stood up and opened the injured book gingerly.

Henry sidled out from under the bed, looking disheveled and annoyed.

"Bad mollymawk," said Strideforth.

Henry clicked his beak and cackled.

"It's nothing to be proud of," Strideforth told him sternly. "You should be ashamed to be so bad."

"Are you hurt?" asked Stella.

"Not really." Strideforth rubbed his cheek. "I'm sorry about your book. Perhaps it can be fixed." He tried to shuffle the torn pages back together. "Henry is very bad." Hortense scowled at him, and he said, "Oh, you know he is, Hortense. He is very, very bad."

Something slipped out from between the pages of the book and fell to the floor. It was the photograph. Stella bent and picked it up.

Strideforth looked at it curiously. "That's here, at Wormwood Mire, isn't it?" he said. "Who are they?"

She showed him the writing on the back. "'P, S and L, Wormwood Mire.' P for Patience." She pointed at the lady in the picture. "That was my mother. And S for Stella. And then L. Maybe my sister? I don't know."

"A sister? Why don't you know?"

Stella gazed at the picture. "I don't remember anything. I was too little."

"Did you live here? But what happened to them?"

"My mother died when I was young. I don't know what happened. My Aunts never answer questions. I do want to find out, though."

"What about your father?" asked Strideforth.

"I don't know." Stella sighed. The only thing she really knew about her father was that the Aunts had disapproved of him. Was it from her father that she had inherited her strange ability to fade and disappear? If he had done anything like that, the Aunts would have been horrified. They detested anything out of the ordinary. She said, "Do you think anyone would remember? Someone who was here about ten years ago?"

"Perhaps Mrs. Burdock might know. But she is always very—"

Suddenly, with a flap of his wings and a triumphant scream, Henry snatched the photograph from Stella's hand.

"No!" she gasped, and tried to tackle him, but he was too quick. He flew up onto the windowsill and then soared away, over the treetops, with the little picture clasped in his beak.

ஐ Six ஐ

Quick!" Strideforth flung open the door. "Come on,"

Stella shoved her bare feet into her boots and laced them up with fumbling fingers. She pulled her coat on over her nightgown and dashed after Strideforth and Hortense, along the passage, down the stairs, along another passage, past the kitchen, and outside into the mist and rain.

In the kitchen yard, an old man was trundling a wheelbarrow full of coal.

"Good morning, Mr. Burdock," Strideforth panted as he ran past. "Did you see—?"

The old man jerked a thumb to the treetops beyond the house and grunted something.

"Thank you."

They raced across the yard, through a broken gate

and the overgrown kitchen garden, between shaggy hedges and flower beds, and around the side of the house to a mossy terrace. A marble gentleman with the tail of a fish reclined in the middle of a stagnant green pond. He looked as if he had once been a fountain, but now he wore a straggling birds' nest on his head as an unlikely hat.

Hortense pointed into the mist.

"There!" said Stella.

Henry was perched at the top of the tallest tree.

"Come on," said Strideforth. They ran down the wide steps from the terrace and across the wet lawn, between the garden beds. Mossy steps led up the hillside. They climbed up, ducking under overhanging branches, pushing through spiky plants. Twigs and thorns caught in Stella's hair. A large plant with leaves like umbrellas arched overhead. Raindrops pattered down.

Stella shoved her way through a particularly prickly bush and found Strideforth and Hortense peering up into the branches of a huge tree. High above, Henry gave a muffled shriek.

The tree towered above them, reaching up into the mist. The trunk was green with moss and tangled with vines. Hortense took off her boots and stockings. She scrambled quickly up the vines, grabbed a branch, and swung herself up like a monkey. She was soon out of sight.

Strideforth pulled off his boots. "Hortense is very good at climbing. She climbed all the cliffs on Tribulation Island to visit the seagulls, and right up the masts on the ship. Right to the top, with the sailors. It will be easier if you take off your boots. You can grip with your toes."

Stella had never climbed a tree. There had been no trees at the Hotel Majestic. She had once climbed out of a third-floor window, but that had been to save her Atlas, and the height had made her dizzy. She unlaced her boots and took them off. She tucked up the skirt of her nightgown. Strideforth clambered up onto a branch and reached down to her. "Come on," he said again.

Stella looked up. Letty wouldn't hesitate. Letty was always brave.

She took a breath, jammed her fingers and toes in between the vines, and started to climb. Strideforth gripped her hand and heaved her up onto the branch. "It is easy," he said. "You'll see. But don't look down."

The branch felt reassuringly solid. Stella pulled herself to her feet and climbed up to the next branch, and then the next.

"Hold on here," said Strideforth. "Put your foot there."

The branches grew close together, rather like a staircase. Stella climbed higher and higher. Dark, prickly leaves scratched her legs and snagged in her hair. Somewhere above, Henry and Hortense were squabbling and shrieking at each other. Stella looked down once, but the glimpse of the ground so far below made her head swim, so she kept her eyes up, gripping with her fingers and toes, pulling herself up with determination from branch to branch, up and up.

When she reached the top of the tree, she was trembling and out of breath. Hortense was sitting on a branch, clutching the photograph to her chest and frowning at Henry. She passed the little picture to Stella.

"Thank you," Stella gasped.

"Bad mollymawk," Strideforth said to Henry.

Henry cackled happily and snapped his beak.

Stella sat cautiously astride a branch. The photograph was battered and bitten and spotted with raindrops, but still in one piece. She flattened it gently and patted it dry as well as she could with the wet hem of her nightgown, and looked at the little faces. One of the babies had almost disappeared. She put the photograph carefully into the pocket of her coat.

It was a strange feeling to be so high up, looking down on everything. She remembered a story from *A Garden of Lilies*. Josephany and Keziah climbed into the low branches of a cherry tree, and later that day were swallowed up unexpectedly by some quicksand.

> *Good girls should never laugh or shout,*
> *Or climb up trees or run about.*

The Aunts would have been horrified had they seen her up here, right at the top of a tall tree, dressed in her nightgown, wet and scratched and muddy.

More than horrified.

But now the Aunts were many, many miles away, and *A Garden of Lilies* had been torn to bits. Cautiously Stella leaned back against the trunk of the tree and swung her bare legs in the cold rain.

Below in the mist were the complicated roofs and towers of Wormwood Mire. Smoke curled up from one of the chimneys. In the yard behind the house, Mr. Burdock looked no bigger than a toy soldier. Three little parrots sped through the trees like green arrows, whistling to one another as they flew.

Strideforth pulled the half-eaten piece of bread

and jam out of his pocket, wiped off some bits of fluff, and took a big bite. He said, pointing, "Look, you can see everything from up here. The railway line and the village. There's the wood. There's the gatehouse, where Mr. and Mrs. Burdock and Jem live. There's the wall. It's very high, with spikes on top, because of all the animals that used to be in the garden. And there's the fernery. And the orchard. And the kitchen garden. And look. Down there is the lake."

Through the branches of the trees and the tangled undergrowth, Stella could see dark water gleaming in the mist, covered with weeds and water lilies.

"Eels and frogs live in there," said Strideforth with his mouth full. "And goldfish. Big ones. It's very overgrown, like a jungle."

Something moved in the water. A dark shape, sliding between the water lilies. Stella gasped. "What was that?"

"What?"

"There. Just there." Stella pointed.

Below, the water lilies shifted, the water swirled and settled.

"A fish?" Strideforth peered down through the branches.

Something splashed, out of sight. From below the surface, a dark shape lunged.

Strideforth pushed the rest of the sandwich into his mouth, clambered farther along the branch, leaned out, nearly lost his balance, yelped, and clutched at the branch. Hortense squeaked. Henry screamed.

Stella grabbed Strideforth's arm and yanked him back.

"Thank you," he said. "Come on." He began to scramble down the tree. "Let's go and see."

Stella followed Strideforth and Hortense down the tree as quickly as she could. She scraped her legs and broke her fingernails. She scrambled down the final few branches and jumped to the ground. Strideforth and Hortense had gone. She could hear them crashing through the bushes. Stella pulled on her boots and followed them down the hillside.

Ferns and creepers grew tall and wild. Stella put her arms over her face and pushed through prickly thickets. She climbed between the low, spreading branches of a tree, ducking under dangling seedpods as large as cucumbers. She struggled through a tangle of clinging vines and came out onto an overgrown path. She stood for a moment, listening for Strideforth and Hortense, but she could only hear raindrops pattering on wet leaves and Henry shrieking somewhere overhead. The path led down toward the lake. She followed it as it wound around rocks and ferns, then through a misty grove of bamboo. She passed a spiky plant growing in an enormous mossy urn. A large snail was making its way along a leaf. Farther on, something gray loomed beside the path. Stella jumped, but it was only the stone statue of a fox, crouched as if it were about to spring.

She took another breath and went on, down steep, mossy steps. Through the undergrowth, she could see glimpses of water. The path came out onto an arched stone bridge.

She leaned on the crumbling parapet. The bank below the bridge was thick with reeds, and farther out, the lake was covered with water lilies. The leaves were larger than dinner plates, curled up at the edges, fringed with spikes. Several flower buds poked up, as big as turnips.

Water trickled from the wide mouth of a mossy marble dolphin. On the other side of the lake stood a little summerhouse like an Egyptian temple. Tendrils of mist drifted. A bubble burst with a sucking, popping sound. From somewhere in the garden came the mournful cry of a peacock. Above the trees was the jagged shape of the tallest tower of Wormwood Mire.

Suddenly something moved. A dark shape sliding through the water lilies.

Stella caught her breath.

A large goldfish jumped from the water and splashed down. The dark shape swam toward it. The gleaming fish jumped again, and then again. The dark shape lunged. Stella gasped. For an instant, the creature's huge head broke the surface of the water. Rows of needlelike teeth glistened in a wide, gulping mouth.

Just as it was almost swallowed, the goldfish made a frantic leap. It flung itself right out of the water and crashed into the reeds below the bridge.

Stella climbed over the parapet and half jumped, half fell down into the reeds. She landed on her hands and knees in the mud and struggled to her feet. She tried not to think of the huge creature in the water nearby.

The reeds rustled. Something slithered.

Heart hammering, Stella said, "Come on," to Letty

and shoved her way through with determination.
She pushed the reeds aside, searching the muddy
ground for the stranded, gasping fish.

She stumbled over a stone and looked down.

She felt her insides lurch.

It was not a stone. It was a stone goldfish.

It lay amongst snapped and broken reeds as if it
had been thrown there. Stella crouched down and
touched it gingerly. It was hard and cold.

A stone goldfish, wet and glistening, mouth gaping, fins outstretched.

Swimming for its life.

ᏚᎧ Seven ᏚᎧᏚ

The stone goldfish was very heavy. Stella staggered as she picked it up. She cradled it in her arms and struggled back through the reeds.

"Stella! Stella! Where are you?"

"Here," she called. "I'm here."

There were crashing sounds in the undergrowth, and then Strideforth and Hortense appeared on the bridge above her. They were scratched and muddy. Strideforth climbed onto the parapet and reached down. Stella scrambled up the bank, clutching the fish awkwardly to her chest. She gripped his hand and clambered back onto the bridge.

"Thank you," she gasped.

He grinned. "We didn't see anything, but we heard something big splashing. A pike, or an eel. Or perhaps a foreign fish. Did you see it?" He noticed the stone goldfish. "What's that?"

Stella told them what she had seen. "It was alive. I saw it jump out of the water," she said. "But when I found it down there, in the reeds, it had turned into stone."

Hortense looked into the stone goldfish's face and made a sad gulping sound to it. Anya darted out, her back arched and her fur standing up in spikes. She squeaked at the fish. Her teeth clicked against stone and she recoiled, chittering angrily.

Strideforth tapped the fish with his finger. "But that is not possible. Fish do not turn into stone."

"I know," said Stella. Of course it was not possible. But all the same, she had seen it happen.

Strideforth shook his head, frowning. "It must be a statue that was lying there. The real goldfish swam away. That is certain. There are statues everywhere in the garden. Look. There's one, just there." He pointed at a small stone turtle at the edge of the water. Farther along the bank was a stone duck.

Stella nodded doubtfully, remembering the huge creature with its wide mouth full of glistening teeth, lurking in the dark water under the weeds and water lilies. She shivered.

Strideforth looked out at the lake for a moment,

then said, "Well, we are very late for breakfast, I think. Are you hungry? Come on."

An overgrown path skirted the edge of the lake, snaking between trees and rocks. They passed the waterfall and found winding steps leading toward the house. Climbing up, they ducked under branches, pushed through clumps of spiky palms and brambles, and emerged onto a terrace above the lake. They crossed an orchard and went along a row of empty stables.

As they reached the kitchen yard, a happy shriek came from somewhere overhead, and Henry sailed down from a chimney stack and landed with a thump on Hortense's head. He clucked at her affectionately.

They stopped to pull off their muddy boots, and Strideforth said, "We must sneak past Mrs. Burdock, if we can. Otherwise there will be trouble."

They looked cautiously in the doorway and tiptoed inside, through the empty kitchen, along the passageway, and up the stairs.

Strideforth peered around the corner of the corridor. "Good. She's not—" Then he gave a gasp and said, "Oh no!"

as a small, elderly woman wearing an apron and an old-fashioned lace cap bustled out of Hortense and Stella's room with a basket of washing.

She gave a squawk. "My heart alive. Look at you. Pingling about like that, out in the mizzle. Wet through. All over with muck. Cold as cabbages." She put down the basket, twitched a towel off the pile of neatly folded washing, and gave Strideforth's wet hair a vigorous rub. "And without your hats. You'll catch your deaths, and serve you right, altogether."

Strideforth emerged from the towel, gasping for breath, his hair sticking up like the crest of a cockatoo. He said, "This is our cousin, Stella. Stella, this is Mrs. Burdock."

Mrs. Burdock gave Stella an odd look, almost as if she were frightened. But then she cleared her throat and said, "Nasty and wet, and still in your nightgown, too!" She saw the stone goldfish in Stella's arms. "And what's that mucky thing you've got there? Are there not enough useless mingle-mangles in this house already?" She wrapped the rough towel around Stella's head and rubbed hard.

"But—" Stella choked, her mouth full of towel.

Mrs. Burdock said, "And you keep right away from that lake, you hear me? You'll get yourself drowned, and then where will you be?" She flapped the towel at Henry, on Hortense's head. "Get away with you, you great grackle." Henry screamed and snapped his beak at her. "None of that," she said, shooing him away. She dried Hortense's hair briskly, ignoring Anya's angry squeaking, and said, "I've unpacked your trunk, Miss Stella, but mind you keep your things tidy. I'm not picking up after you."

"Has the postman come today?" asked Strideforth.

"If he comes, I'll tell you, Master Strideforth," said Mrs. Burdock. She gave him a push toward his bedroom and bustled Stella and Hortense into theirs, clucking angrily. "Come on with you, now. Out of those nasty wet clothes."

As Stella pulled her nightgown off over her head, she remembered what Strideforth had said about the photograph. She took a breath and said, "Please, Mrs. Burdock. Do you remember a lady who stayed here about ten years ago? She had two babies." She took the photograph from the pocket of her coat. "This lady."

Mrs. Burdock stared at the little picture. She put her hand to her mouth. After a moment, she said, "My heart alive. Why would you be asking me a thing like that?"

"She was my mother. I think I was one of the babies," said Stella.

Mrs. Burdock opened her mouth, then shut it again. She gave Stella another odd look. Then she frowned and said, "No. No. I don't know nothing about that. Nothing at all."

"But—" said Stella.

"Ask no questions, hear no lies," snapped Mrs. Burdock. "Get on with you. Get yourselves washed and dry and respectable, altogether. As much use as tadpoles in a trifle, you are." She bundled up their wet clothes and went away, muttering to herself.

The remains of *A Garden of Lilies* lay on the dressing table. Stella looked at the photograph again. *I will find out what happened,* she told the three pale faces. She tucked the little picture safely back between the torn pages and put the heavy stone goldfish on top of the book. It sat there, fins outstretched, still and cold. Could it really have been swimming in the lake only a short time before? That seemed very unlikely. It looked exactly like a garden ornament.

Strideforth was right. It was impossible.

Hortense touched the fish with her finger. Anya hissed at it, her fur bristling.

Stella washed her hands and face. Shivering, she found clean drawers, a vest, a pair of woolen stockings, two petticoats, and a dress in the wardrobe, and pulled them on. She twisted around but could not reach all the long row of tiny buttons down the back of the dress. "Could you help me, please?" she asked Hortense.

The little girl was putting on dry stockings. She scowled, but came over and fastened the buttons neatly.

"Thank you." Stella dragged the brush through her wet, tangled hair and plaited it again. As she tied a ribbon at the end of the plait, she saw in the mirror that Hortense was watching her.

"Would you like me to brush your hair?" Stella asked.

Hortense frowned and shook her head.

⁓⁓⁓

Miss Araminter looked up from her book as they came into the kitchen and said, "There you are, my dears. Good morning."

Mrs. Burdock bustled in, carrying their wet clothes in a washing basket. She said, "Out in the rain, they were. Climbing trees and jumping in the lake, or some foolishness. Trailing muck and weeds into the house. Making work for people. It ain't respectable. More trouble than grasshoppers in the gravy. If they were mine, ma'am, I'd give them what for."

Miss Araminter smiled vaguely and picked a twig out of Hortense's tangled hair, which made Anya spit and hiss. "The giant spruce," she said. "*Picea giganteum.* A magnificent specimen, as I am sure you will agree, Mrs. Burdock. From the Americas, and at least eighty years old, I should think. The leaves are useful for scurvy and blackwater fever."

Mrs. Burdock looked annoyed. "That's all very fine, I'm sure, ma'am. All that reading of yours. But sense is sense. They say the old gent spent days locked up in that library of his, all them years ago, reading. Or down in that summerhouse. Up to no good, no doubt. When he wasn't bringing useless piles of piffle back from foreign parts for other folk to dust. What's the point of it? That's what I'd like to know." She gave an angry snort and added, "And that dratted boy of mine's late back from the village again. Firtling about, no doubt. I'll give him the back of my hand, I will." She picked up the laundry basket and went away.

❧

After breakfast (bread and jam and cocoa), Miss Araminter smiled and rubbed her hands together. "Lessons," she said, and cleared a space at the end of the kitchen table. She presented Stella with a smart blue notebook and two sharp pencils, a piece of India rubber, a pen, and six shiny nibs in a little tin.

The first lesson was botany, and Miss Araminter told them many interesting facts about the giant sundews of Malacca. Stella carefully copied a picture of a giant sundew into her new notebook with one of her new pencils and labeled all the different parts of it, in English and also in Latin.

After the botany lesson came mathematics. Stella had learned only simple arithmetic from the Aunts, and she worked carefully through the sums that Miss Araminter set her, counting on her fingers. Anya made inky footprints between 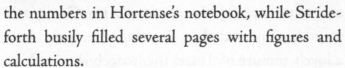 the numbers in Hortense's notebook, while Strideforth busily filled several pages with figures and calculations.

Then came more botany. They learned about buttercups (the roots were useful for raising blisters), the enormous St. Thomas bean (which grew so large that the individual beans could be used as snuffboxes) and some of the carnivorous lilies of the Congo. Stella made a drawing in her notebook of a Congolese lily swallowing a mouse.

Next came Latin. Henry had been sleeping on

the mantelpiece, but when the Latin lesson began, he woke up with a happy shriek. He flapped to the table and landed with a thump that knocked a bottle of ink onto the floor.

Strideforth hurled his Latin primer at the bird. It missed, but Henry screamed and nearly toppled off the table. He grabbed the book in his beak and tried to tear it apart.

"No," said Miss Araminter.

Henry screamed, "*Stulte!*"

Miss Araminter snatched the book back. "Behave yourself," she said.

Stella caught Hortense's eye and giggled. Hortense gave her a tiny smile.

After Latin came botany, a short break for cocoa and some caraway biscuits from a tin, Greek, still more botany, and then drawing. Hortense drew a lovely picture of Teasel the hedgehog crunching up a beetle, and Miss Araminter pinned it on the wall.

They had dinner (bread and cheese and apples and walnuts), and then Miss Araminter gave Strideforth a list of the members of the nightshade family to learn and a Latin lesson to study. She gave Hortense a page of sums to complete and an enormous prickly thistle to draw. She gave Stella a piece of paper, an envelope, and a penny stamp, to write a letter to the Aunts. Then she smiled and wished them a pleasant afternoon, picked up a pair of clippers and a basket, put on her coat and hat, clasped her umbrella, and strode outside into the rain.

❧ *Eight* ❧

S tella dipped her pen into the ink and paused. In *A Garden of Lilies*, Lucretia made a blot on a letter she was writing to her godmother and was squashed unexpectedly by a falling bust of Prince Albert.

> *Be attentive when you write,*
> *Or you might not make it through the night.*

Rather discouraged by this depressing story, Stella wrote very carefully:

> *Dear Aunts,*

She stopped and gazed around the warm kitchen. The fire hissed in the grate and the heating pipes clanked overhead. Strideforth was kicking the leg of his chair and filling the margin of his Latin primer with diagrams of cogs and wheels and steam pipes. Hortense was drawing the thistle, the tip of her tongue poking out in concentration. Anya was pouncing on a piece of India rubber. Henry was snoring loudly on the mantelpiece, his head tucked under his wing. Stella chewed the end of her pen for a bit, and then wrote:

I hope this letter finds you in tolerable health.

What to put next? The Aunts were very particular about letters. She imagined Aunt Deliverance opening the envelope in the breakfast room of the Hotel Majestic and glaring at the letter with her beady black eyes. Stella thought for a few minutes, and then dipped the pen into the ink again and wrote:

I had an agreeable journey and arrived at Wormwood Mire last evening.

What next? She couldn't tell the Aunts about what Henry had done to *A Garden of Lilies*, or about climbing the tree, or about the dark shape swimming in the lake, or about the stone goldfish.

> *My cousins' governess is a very educated lady,*
> *and we are studying Latin and mathematics*
> *and drawing and botany.*

Surely the Aunts would approve of all these lessons. Stella looked at her inky fingers and thought about the creature in the lake. She had only glimpsed it for a moment. Was it a pike or an eel, as Strideforth thought? Or some kind of foreign fish? She remembered the huge dark head and the gaping mouth full of pointed teeth. Perhaps Miss Araminter knew about fish. Or maybe there was a book about them in the library. A book about foreign fish would be an agreeable replacement for *A Garden of Lilies.*

Before she could think of anything else to write, Anya jumped sideways, twisting like a snake, and made a loud, chittering noise. Cheerful, piercing whistling and clattering footsteps came from outside. Henry woke up, shrieked, and flapped his wings.

"It's Jem," said Strideforth with a grin.

A small, skinny boy poked his head around the door. He was about the same age as Hortense, with a freckled face and carrot-colored hair. "Granny ain't here?" he asked in a whisper.

Strideforth shook his head.

The boy sidled in. He wore a large, shabby oilskin coat dripping with water, and carried a basket and a can of milk. He set them down with a thump and stretched his arms. Anya dashed toward him, hissing, her fur spiky.

"She's right fierce, ain't she?" he said admiringly. "I got her something." He fished a little piece of cheese out of his pocket and held it out. Anya edged forward, snatched up the cheese, and darted up to Hortense's shoulder. She perched there and ate the cheese, holding it in both hands like a squirrel. Jem watched her, grinning.

Strideforth said, "This is our cousin, Stella. Stella, this is Jem Burdock."

"Good afternoon," said Stella.

"G'afternoon, miss," he said. He took a large loaf of bread from the basket and put it on the table. "I'm that late back again. Granny'll skin me alive if she sees me. She's got a toothache, and she's been cross as a bear for weeks. She says I wouldn't be late if I din't hang around listening to gossip. 'Keep your nose out and your mouth shut,' that's what she always says." He looked over his shoulder, then leaned forward, lowered his voice, and added, "Tom Pintucket, in the village, reckons he seen the monster again, last night. Clear as day. Everyone's talking about it."

"A monster!" said Stella.

"Tom says it were right there"—Jem jerked a thumb over his shoulder—"in North Field, right near Boggart Wood. Like a shadow, he says. And glinting. That's the second time he seen it. He says it's back."

"There's no such thing as monsters," said Strideforth, frowning.

"Well, it ain't been around for years and years. Since afore I was born. When I were little, Granny used to tell me, 'Finish your porridge or the monster'll gobble you up.'" Jem laughed. "But Tom had three sheep gone, night before last. Nothing left, not even a scrap of wool. Tom reckons the monster crunched them up, bones and all. He reckons it's back, for sure. And Mrs. Thorn's little ginger cat's gone too. Although that might've just wandered off." Jem gave a sudden bloodthirsty grin. "It must be a cobbin' great thing to eat up three sheep. I'd like to see that, I would."

Strideforth said, "Probably those sheep were taken by thieves. There were many bandits in the Argentine. They steal cattle and shoot people. They would steal sheep, too, that is certain."

Jem shrugged. "I reckon it lives in Boggart Wood, most likely, and comes out at night. Maybe it's a panther, escaped from a fair. Maybe it's a huge big badger. A huge big sheep-eating badger!"

"Where's Boggart Wood?" asked Stella.

"It's close by here, miss." Jem pointed. "You can see it from the road, down in the valley. It's right creepy. Granny says keep to the road, don't go near the wood, but I've been down there, I have. There's an old cart track goes down, near the bridge. I ain't frit of nothing. I've been close, but I ain't been in. You have to be careful, miss. Because if you go in the wood, you might get lost and never come out again. There are caves under there. The stream drops right down into a hole and goes underground. And there's a ghost in there too. And some people say there's a ruined castle in there, that giants built in the old days."

"There's no such thing as giants," said Strideforth, "or ghosts either."

"There is a ghost," said Jem. "It's a ghost of a girl. A singing girl. People say you can hear it singing to itself in the night, right in the middle of the wood, near the crossroads. If you hear it, it means something bad will happen to you." He leaned on the table. "There's ghosts all over. There's this one ghost on the highway, over near Brockley. It's a black dog, big as a calf. People say if you're walking there just at dusk, you feel its breath on the back of your neck, warmlike. But you mustn't turn around. You just keep walking. Because if you turn around and look in its eyes, you die of fright. Mrs. Gromwell's granny felt its breath one time, and she was right peculiar after that, so they say." He grinned again. "And there's a coach and four that comes over the bridge at Cobden Wake at midnight. That's a ghost too. Them ghost horses ain't got no heads. And them ghost coachmen ain't got none either. No heads at all." He laughed. "I'd like to see that, I would."

Strideforth said, "Those are just stories to frighten little children. There aren't any ghosts. And there aren't any giants or monsters, either. You should not believe foolish things like that."

Jem laughed again. "Lots of folk say that. And Granny says, what with Tom drinking in the Leopard every night, ain't no wonder he's seein' things in the wood. That's what Granny says. But she makes Granda lock the hens away and puts the shutters up at nightfall all the same. I seen him. Everyone's frit.

They're locking up tight and staying in after dark, whatever they say."

Stella asked, "Aren't you scared?"

Jem said, "I ain't frit of the monster. I ain't frit of nothing. I'm going to be a sailor when I grow up, like my da. And sailors are right brave. And I know how to keep safe. I whistle if I go near the wood. Whistling keeps you safe from ghosts, and maybe from monsters, too, I reckon. And I wear this red hanky round my neck, that's lucky. And my shirt outside in, like this, so I can't be tricked off the path by nothing. And look, I got a tallybag." He pulled out a bootlace from around his neck. A little bag hung from it, bound tightly with red thread. "It's got a hazel twig in it, and a bit of bread, and an iron nail from a horseshoe, and a scrip of proper black writing from the Bible."

"That's just superstition," said Strideforth. "A little bag can't protect you from anything."

"So you say, Master Strideforth. But I know it works, because I've been right close to Boggart Wood, close enough to spit, and I'm safe, ain't I? And you can't argue with that. I got it off Mrs. Spindleweed, at the sweetshop. And it cost me a bob, so it's a good 'un." Jem tucked the little bag back under his shirt and gave it a pat. "Mrs. Spindleweed's right clever. She fixed my granda's arm up when he burned it, better'n new, he says. But she gives me the shivers. Everyone's frit of her."

Stella remembered Mrs. Spindleweed's strange yellow eyes. She said, "I was in the sweetshop yesterday. It was a bit—" She hesitated. "I heard an owl, I think."

Jem nodded. "She's got a huge big owl. I've seen it flying in her window. Mrs. Spindleweed can put a shadow after you in your dreams so you can't never sleep the night through. She put a chill on George Oakapple one time. He were in bed for a week, shaking with cold. And she can make you hurt yourself, without even coming near." He lowered his voice again and said, "And they say she's got a familiar."

"What's a familiar?" asked Stella.

Jem looked over his shoulder. "It's a little thing. You can't see it, but it can see you. It might be right beside you, but you wouldn't know. Sometimes you can hear her talking to it, inside the sweetshop. But there ain't nobody there. Nobody that you can see, anyways. They say she found it in Boggart Wood, and she caught it, and now it runs errands for her."

Stella felt the back of her neck prickle, but Strideforth laughed and said, "That's all nonsense."

"It ain't lucky to joke about things like that, Master Strideforth," Jem said seriously. "You've got to be careful. And I reckon the monster's back, whatever you say. Because them three sheep din't just wander off. They got took, that's for sure. Took by something."

"But not by a monster," said Strideforth.

Stella said, "You don't know. There might be a monster. There might be anything. We saw something swimming in the lake today."

"That was just a big fish. Maybe an eel," said Strideforth.

Jem grinned. "There's big 'uns down in that lake. Grown big since the old gent died. They'd be great-great-grandfather fish by now." He laughed. "I'd go fishing there, I would. I'd catch something big. But Granny says she'll clobber me if I go near the lake. Granda says when the old gent was alive fifty years back, there used to be a rhinoserry and giraffes and a crocodrill here in the garden. All kinds of foreign creatures. He saw them when he was a little lad. I wish I'd seen them. Twenty servants, the old gent had, Granda says, and more for parties. They could see the fireworks and hear the music all the way in the village. The old gent went all round the world, he did. And he came back here to live when he was old. But he was right strange, from being in foreign parts for so long. Granda says he used to dress up like a Turk and drive two of them black-and-white foreign horses. You know, stripy like humbugs."

"Zebras," said Stella.

"Zebras." Jem nodded. "And wild. There was three men in the forge back then, and all together they couldn't shoe any of 'em. Them zebras wouldn't have it. Not them. Kicking and biting and all. But they're all gone. There ain't nothing like that left here now. Nothing at all. Excepting them parrots, and them bats, and them peacocks, screeching all the time."

"Do you know about someone who stayed here, about ten years ago?" Stella asked. "A lady? With two little babies?"

Jem shrugged. "I don't know, miss. That was afore I was born. This house's been empty for years an' years. People used to come sometimes, but they din't stay long. I'll ask Granny if you like?"

"Yes, please," said Stella.

"I will, then." He picked up the basket. "Anyway, I'm off, afore she catches me. I'm meant to be weeding the cabbages." He laughed. "G'afternoon, Master Strideforth, Miss Stella, Miss Hortense." They heard his boots clattering and his cheerful whistling as he crossed the yard outside.

"It's all just stories, you know," Strideforth said as he carried the loaf of bread and the can of milk away to the larder. He came back and added, "There are no such things as monsters or ghosts. That is certain. Jem should not believe in all that nonsense."

Stella imagined the monster, hiding in the dark wood, gnawing on the bones of the missing sheep.

Strideforth sat down at the table and opened his Latin primer again. He stared at the page for a few minutes, and then drew some more steam pipes in the margin. He hummed to himself for a bit, rocked his chair back, and looked at the pipes that snaked across the ceiling, hissing and clanking. He said, "They go all around this house. Some of them are hot, but most of them are cold. The furnace burns a lot of coal. The heat must be going somewhere." He slammed his Latin primer shut. "I'm just going to have a look," he said, and left the room.

Stella stared at her letter. It was extremely short, and the Aunts would certainly disapprove of it. She gazed into space for several minutes but could not think of anything else to write. Hortense was still drawing the thistle. Anya was draped across the back of her neck, sleeping. Henry was snoring on the mantelpiece. The clock ticked. The heating pipes clanked. Raindrops pattered against the windows.

Stella wrote:

It is raining today.

After a few moments, she added:

Perhaps it will be fine tomorrow.

Suddenly the door banged open and Strideforth came bounding back into the room. "Stella, have you finished your letter? I've found something to show you."

"What is it?"

He grinned. "It's a surprise. You'll see. Bring that photograph with the babies in it. Come on."

Stella dipped the pen into the ink and wrote:

Yours dutifully,
Stella Montgomery

She blotted the letter quickly, folded it, pushed it into the envelope, and wrote the address on the front:

The Misses Montgomery
Hotel Majestic
Withering-by-Sea

She licked the stamp, stuck it on, and tucked the letter safely under a heavy black stone.

~✧~ Nine ~✧~

*E*ven in the daytime, the house was shadowy. Stella followed Strideforth along the dusty passageways.

They passed the portrait of Wilberforce Montgomery, and Stella stopped to have another look at him. His little black boot-button eyes reminded her of Aunt Deliverance, but that was the only resemblance, because his expression was rather cheerful. He was sitting in the little Egyptian summerhouse down beside the lake, surrounded by books and plants and animals. Behind him, swans glided between tidy clumps of water lilies, and beyond that, the neat garden sloped steeply up toward Wormwood Mire. The painting was cracked and green with mildew, but Stella could see a group of kangaroos and a camel grazing beside an ornate fountain and a giraffe standing in a flower bed. Parrots and monkeys perched on clipped hedges, decorative urns, and the branches of the trees.

The other paintings along the passageway were of ships and foreign towns and tropical fish and porcupines and toucans. There were several more of Wilberforce Montgomery. In one, he was standing proudly with his arm around a rhinoceros. In another, he was driving a smart carriage pulled by zebras along a busy city street. In a third, he was riding a yak and smiling off into the distance. He wore an enormous furry hat decorated with beads and feathers. Behind him, towering mountains reached up into the sky.

Strideforth felt a heating pipe. He followed it along the wall, crouched down, and rapped it with his knuckles. "Cold," he said. He stood up. "Come on. It's upstairs."

In the entrance hall, the gold wallpaper gleamed in the shadows. Strideforth led the way up the curving staircase, and then up a second flight of stairs and along a passageway lined with doors. He tapped the heating pipes. "These are all cold too," he said. "I don't understand. The heat must be going somewhere. It's all bedrooms up here." At the end of the passage, he pushed open a door. "Look. It's in here."

The room was a nursery, with whitewashed walls and bars on the windows. A rusty fireguard stood in front of the empty grate. A narrow iron bed was covered with a dust sheet. There were two small cots, a white-painted wardrobe, a wooden rocking chair, and a wooden screen covered with pasted pictures of flowers and animals and children. Water dripped from the ceiling and made puddles on the cracked linoleum.

In a corner of the room was an old-fashioned perambulator. Strideforth pointed. "It's the one in the photograph, isn't it?"

Stella gasped. "Yes." She compared it with the little photograph. "Yes, it is."

He grinned. "I thought so."

The leather was torn and the iron spokes of the wheels were rusty. Stella touched the wooden handle. Had she sat in here with Letty? Two babies, bundled up in quilts and blankets as their mother pushed them around the overgrown garden?

"Do you remember it?" asked Strideforth.

Stella shook her head sadly. "No. I don't remember anything."

She looked around the room. It was shabby and neglected. Had she once slept here?

She pulled open the wardrobe door. A clutter of rubbish lay on a bottom shelf. She crouched down and poked around. Moldy cleaning rags, an empty medicine bottle, and a few painted building blocks.

Beside one of the windows was the wooden rocking chair. Strideforth gave it a push, and it creaked back and forth.

Something flickered at the back of Stella's mind. Sunlight shimmering . . .

"I remember that chair, I think," she said slowly. "I remember someone sitting right there."

"They must have been waiting for someone to come," said Strideforth.

"Waiting? Why?"

"You would sit here and wait for a visitor. That's the drive, down there." He pointed toward the window. "You would sit right here and watch for people to arrive."

Stella pushed the dusty curtain aside, leaned on the windowsill, and looked out. Raindrops trickled down the glass. Below, the drive curved around toward the front door of the house. Strideforth was right. From here, you would see anyone who arrived.

Stella pushed the curtain farther back. "Look," she

said. Hidden in the corner of the windowsill was a little wooden box.

She wiped dust from it. It was about three inches square and decorated with a twining pattern of flowers made out of tiny pieces of wood of different colors, red like autumn leaves, glossy chestnut brown, gleaming black, and as pale as moonlight. Stella polished it with her sleeve. Little mother-of-pearl butterflies were scattered in between the flowers. They glinted as if they were fluttering. It was quite beautiful.

Curving across the lid of the box in silver letters was the name *Patience*. Above the name, almost hidden amongst the flowers and butterflies, were a tiny silver star and a tiny silver moon.

"Patience," Stella whispered. She traced the letters, her finger trembling. "Patience. My mother. This must have been hers."

"What's inside?"

Stella held her breath and opened the lid.

"Oh," she said, disappointed. The box contained only a dried flower and a tiny strip of curled paper. She picked up the flower, but it was so fragile it crumbled into dust. She uncurled the little piece of paper. It had faint writing on it. She read out, "'Crossroads. Midnight. I will wait.'"

Strideforth said, "A message. What crossroads? Midnight is a strange time to meet someone."

Stella read the message again and shook her head. "I don't know."

She closed the box and ran her finger along the silver letters again. She had never held anything that had belonged to her mother. She stroked the smooth wood. Her fingers found a little round hole at the back, hidden in the pattern.

Strideforth examined it. "It's a keyhole," he said. He opened the lid and looked inside. He turned the box over and tapped it underneath. "A secret compartment, do you think? There must be a key somewhere."

They looked along the windowsill. Stella shook the curtains, dislodging years of dust and several large moths. They searched the floor. Stella peeled back the cracked linoleum and spied something gleaming, wedged tight in the gap between two floorboards.

"I'll get it out." Strideforth opened his pocket-knife. "Father gave us some money to spend in London. I bought this." He showed Stella the knife and selected a short, pointed blade. He poked it into the gap between the floorboards. "It has fifteen different blades. There's one to take stones out of horses' hooves, and one to open tins, and one to sharpen pencils, and one to curl a mustache, and one to adjust a lady's corset in an emergency. It's very, very useful. There." He grinned and passed Stella a tiny silver key.

It fitted the keyhole. Stella pushed it in and turned it. The key went around and around, clicking, like winding a watch. She opened the lid of the box and tinkling music poured out. A whispering, melancholy tune, like raindrops falling on wet leaves. Stella caught her breath. She had the strangest feeling, as if she had heard this music before. A long time ago.

Something stirred at the back of her mind like a distant, flickering light.

Sunlight shimmering . . .

All at once she remembered sitting on the floor of the nursery. Right here. With her sister. They had a little wooden doll each. Her doll had a pink dress, and her sister's had a yellow one. Her sister was chewing her doll's head. Soon it would have no hair left at all.

Their mother sat in the ROcking chair beside the window. She was thin and pale and sad, and she wore a gray gown. She sat and rocked and sang along to the whispering, tinkling music, and looked out the window.

She was crying.

Stella held her breath. In her memory, she saw the

sunlight slanting in through the window. The shimmering light seemed to pass right through her and her sister, as if they were floating, hazy and insubstantial as smoke. Stella blinked, watching the glinting specks of dust dancing in the sunlight.

The musical box wound down. The image shone in her memory, fading as the music slowed.

The music stopped. The memory glimmered and dissolved and was gone.

Raindrops ran down the window.

"They were here," Stella said. "I remember them. My mother. And my sister. And me." She looked around the empty, shadowy room. "I remember. We were right here." She wiped a tear that had trickled down her cheek.

Strideforth said, "You're sad."

"No, not really." Stella smiled. "I wish—" She stopped. She was not sure what she wished. She thought of her mother, sitting in the rocking chair, looking out at the drive. Watching and waiting and crying. She remembered playing in the sunshine with her sister. With Letty.

Stella put the silver key and the little photograph inside the musical box. She touched the three tiny faces with the tip of her finger and gently closed the lid.

✂ Ten ✂

Strideforth said, "Why was your mother here, anyway? It is strange to be staying in a big empty house, don't you think?"

Stella nodded, turning the musical box over in her hands. "It is strange." She thought for a moment. "I'm here now because my Aunts sent me away. They were very angry."

Strideforth said, "Father sent us away." He paused. "He was angry too."

Stella looked around the neglected nursery and thought about what Ada had said at the railway station. Had her mother been sent to stay in this empty house because she had done something wrong? Was that why she had been crying?

Strideforth said, "And I think Father must still be angry with us. Because he has not sent us a letter.

Not one. There is a ship every month. If he had writ-ten to us, we would have the letter by now. Two let-ters. Maybe he's forgotten us."

Strideforth looked miserable. Stella patted his arm and tried to think of something comforting to say. "Sometimes letters are late. Or they get lost."

He nodded, sniffed, and rubbed his face with the back of his hand. "Come on," he said. "Let's see what else we can find. Perhaps you will remember some-thing more."

Stella pushed the musical box into her pocket, and they searched the nursery for clues. Stride-forth crawled under the bed. Stella looked along the windowsills, behind the curtains. Strideforth scrabbled around and came out backward, covered with dust, clutching only a bent teaspoon and a dead beetle. Stella pushed the perambulator across the room, clambered up onto it, balanced unsteadily, and groped around on top of the wardrobe. Stride-forth tried unsuccessfully to prize up a floorboard with his pocketknife. He pulled the fireguard aside, climbed into the grate, and looked up the chimney. He emerged covered with soot, sneezed, and said, "Nothing."

They wandered back along the passageway and searched the other bedrooms. They pulled open wardrobe doors and peered under beds. Stella found a shoe with a tarnished buckle and a chamber pot containing three dead snails. In a wardrobe, she discovered several old-fashioned coats, a broken fan made of ostrich feathers, and a bonnet decorated with moldy silk violets. Strideforth put on the bonnet. It came down over his eyes. He opened the fan and waved it around in an elegant manner, shedding several feathers. Stella giggled.

Outside, the rain was becoming heavier and the wind was blowing in gusts. Something rattled against the roof.

Strideforth investigated the bathroom. "If the furnace was working properly, we might have hot baths up here," he said, inspecting the enamel tub, which held several inches of stagnant green water. He tapped the pipes and lifted the heavy mahogany lid of the lavatory and peered inside. The glazed china bowl was painted with flowers and leaves. He pulled the chain and there was a clanking sound, but nothing happened. He climbed up and poked around in the cistern.

"Do you remember anything?" Strideforth asked as he clambered down, dripping slightly.

Stella looked along the shadowy passageway. "No. Nothing at all," she said.

"Let's try downstairs," said Strideforth. "We should look in all the rooms. You might recognize something."

They went back down to the entrance hall and wandered on, in and out of the dark rooms. Bulky pieces of furniture were covered with dust sheets, making strange, looming shapes. "Billiard room, Turkish smoking room, gun room, Japanese drawing room," said Strideforth. He pushed open a door. "Here's the library."

It was a shadowy room with a high ceiling. The walls were lined with bookcases made of dark wood, carved with patterns of vines and leaves. Overhead was an iron gallery and more bookcases. The shelves reached all the way up to the ceiling, which was painted like the night sky, scattered with stars. The windows were hung with tattered velvet curtains. Some of the glass panes were broken, and tendrils of ivy snaked in from outside.

Strideforth felt a heating pipe and frowned. He rapped it with his knuckles. "These are hot. Where do they go?" He peered up at the ceiling. There was a faint humming sound from somewhere overhead.

Stella looked around at the shelves. There were hundreds of books. Some were bound with dark leather and had gold writing on their spines. Some

had lost their covers and were just sad bundles of damp paper. She chose one and opened it. The pages were spotted with mildew and black with jagged, foreign print. Perhaps this was Latin, and if she studied with Strideforth, she would be able to read it.

The next book she chose was full of large holes like a Swiss cheese, as if it had been eaten by something. Perhaps by a large, poisonous invertebrate. Stella shuddered and put it gingerly back on the shelf.

Strideforth said, "Do you want to look at the books? I'm going to follow these pipes and see where they come from. I won't be long. I'll come straight back."

The library seemed more shadowy when Strideforth had gone. Stella wound up the musical box, put it on a shelf, and opened the lid. The melancholy, tinkling music played as she wandered along the shelves, looking at the books. At the back of her mind, she remembered the sunny nursery again. It was comforting to think of her mother and Letty, here at the house, all those years ago. She found a large volume of sermons, which seemed both difficult and dull, and a book about weights and measures, and one that contained descriptions of battles from obscure foreign wars.

The musical box ran down and stopped, and Stella wound it up again. She found a book of French poems and managed to puzzle out a few words. Steam pipes hissed and clanked. Overhead, something still hummed, like a fly caught in a bottle.

Stella pushed the book back into place and gazed around at the shelves, feeling a bit discouraged. Surely, after traveling the world, Wilberforce Montgomery should have had a more interesting library.

In a dark corner, a spiral staircase led up to the gallery. She closed the musical box and put it back into her pocket before climbing the stairs.

The humming sound was becoming louder. Stella threaded her way between stacks of books, boxes, piles of paper, and other rubbish. She poked into a wooden crate and found the broken pieces of a green egg that must have been the size of a cocoa-nut, the skeleton of a mouse, and several desiccated moths.

The humming had become a rattling buzz. Stella reached the end of the gallery and looked at the final bookcase. It held a jumble of books, two cardboard boxes, and a dead spider. Cautiously, she opened one of the boxes and found a large, moldy bird's nest. The other box contained a collection of decaying seaweed.

Stella stood and listened. The buzzing sound seemed to come from inside the wall, as if an insect were trapped behind the shelves.

She tapped the back of the bookcase. It sounded hollow.

She gave the bookcase a push. It creaked and shifted. From behind the shelves came a frantic burst of buzzing and banging.

She pulled all the books from the shelves, piled them on the floor, and examined the empty bookcase carefully. Vines and leaves were carved all around the edges of the shelves. She ran her fingers along the wood. It was smooth and felt slightly warm. Her fingers found a carved snake hidden amongst the vines. It twined around the foliage, and its head stuck out between the leaves. She grasped it with both hands and tried to twist it one way and then the other. Something moved. Then there was a loud creak. Stella jumped back nervously. Would it crash down on top of her?

When nothing happened, she shoved the

bookcase as hard as she could. It creaked again, and then swung slowly back, revealing a dark space.

A swarm of insects hurtled out in a gust of warm air. They surrounded her head, buzzing and clicking, battering her face with their tiny wings.

They flew so fast they seemed like streaks of light. They gleamed like sweets wrappers, green and blue and silver. One hovered for a second. Stella reached out a hand and felt the air prickle. There was a spark and a flash.

"Ouch!" Stella rubbed her tingling fingers together.

The insects circled the shadowy library, sparking and hissing like the flames of damp candles. They blundered into the windows and the bookshelves and buzzed around and around the chandelier, crackling with electricity. One of them found a broken windowpane and disappeared into the garden. The others followed. They swarmed around the window and then, one by one, they darted away through the broken glass and out into the rain. One flew back and buzzed three times around Stella's head, sending out tiny sparks that made her flinch and blink. It hovered in front of her face, making a high-pitched, clicking sound, and then it darted away, out of the window, and was gone.

Stella rubbed her fingers together again and caught her breath. Her hair felt as if it were standing on end, and the air smelled of burning paper. She peered into the space that had opened up behind the bookcase. What else was in there? It was very dark. Perhaps she should wait for Strideforth to return before investigating.

She remembered a story from *A Garden of Lilies*. On a trip to the seaside, Maurice, Netty, and Obadiah ventured into the mouth of a cave and were dragged into an enormous whirlpool.

> *Curiosity killed the cat,*
> *And you as well. Be sure of that.*

Stella sighed. *A Garden of Lilies* was very discouraging.

She shoved a box against the bookcase to prevent it from closing, took a determined breath, and stepped into darkness.

Eleven

The narrow passageway was musty and warm. Stella felt her way along cautiously. Wispy, trailing fingers brushed against her face. Her outstretched hands found a tangle of cobwebs. She pushed her way through the sticky threads with a shudder.

The passageway turned a corner, went along for a bit, turned another corner, and then ended. Stella groped around in the darkness and stumbled against steep wooden stairs. She began to climb. The stairs twisted and turned, came to a little landing, and led up again. Light filtered down from above.

She reached the top of the stairs and found herself in a small, eight-sided room lined with crowded shelves. Heating pipes coiled up from below, clanking and hissing and emitting little bursts of steam.

The air was hot and humid. Rain pattered against the narrow windows.

Stella looked around. The shelves were crammed full of things. Fossils and huge eggs and strange bones and pieces of branching coral and long, curling feathers and enormous, gleaming beetles. A spindly crab with legs almost a yard long hung from the ceiling, next to a small stuffed crocodile. There was a telescope and a sextant and a butterfly net and a pith helmet. A dead vine emerged from a large pot, scrambled up the shelves, and snaked across the ceiling. Several brown leaves and dry seedpods dangled overhead.

There were rows and rows of books: *Mythical Beasts of Mandalay*, *Night Creatures of the Feejee Islands*, *Terrifying Travels in Tartary*. A globe of the world stood in a corner. A cage held the skeleton of a small creature. It was difficult to say what it had been. It had the head and wings of a bird and the tail of a snake. In a glass tank was a cluster of large cocoons, and there were several more dangling from the underside of shelves and from the windowsills. Stella touched one gingerly with her finger. It was empty and as dry as paper. Whatever had been inside had hatched and gone.

A desk sat in the center of the room, cluttered with papers. In the middle lay a fat leather-bound book.

Its cover was so gouged and battered and stained that it looked as if it had been attacked by a savage animal. And then dropped in a puddle. It was tied together with a piece of cord. Stella brushed dust from the cover and undid the knot. She opened the book. On the first page was written, in extravagant, looping handwriting, *A Journal of the Ramblings and Collectings of Wilberforce Montgomery.*

She turned a few pages and read: *I had been paddling cautiously along the shore, when suddenly a huge Crocodile rushed from the reeds as swift as an arrow, with a Tremendous Roar and open Jaws, belching Water and Smoke that fell upon me like rain in a Hurricane.*

Stella sat down on the desk chair. The pages of the journal were crumpled and torn, and Wilberforce Montgomery's handwriting was old-fashioned and sprawling and difficult to read. In some places, the ink had faded to the color of weak tea. An account of a visit to a castle in Roumania had been spattered with a dark liquid, and toward the end, the only sentence Stella could decipher was, *I was Fortunate indeed to escape with my Life.* On the next page, he was traveling through a sandstorm in the Sahara. Two recipes, one for boot polish, which included soot and champagne, and another for the treatment of a camel with dropsy, were scribbled onto the back of an invitation to a dance in Timbuktu. Further on, she found a description of the difficulties of bringing home a number of reptile eggs and a collection of tropical plants, including a large tank containing a giant water lily. He packed straw and hot-water bottles around the eggs, as the ship in which he was traveling nearly foundered off Cape Horn in an icy storm. This story ended abruptly—several pages had been torn out—and Stella could not find what happened next.

On the following page was a drawing of a cocoon, like the empty ones in the tank on the shelf.

Traveling through these Islands, I encountered a colony of Lightning Beetles, and despite painful stings and shocks from the Creatures, which displayed remarkable intelligence, I managed to collect several Cocoons. If they survive the journey and hatch outside the Tropics, they will be a Diverting Addition to my Secret Collection.

There was a picture of one of the insects that had flown out of the hidden passage into the library. Stella looked at the empty cocoons in the tank. Clearly,

the beetles had survived the journey and multiplied. And now that the furnace was going again and the study was as warm as the tropics, they had hatched once more and had been buzzing around the room, trying to escape.

She turned a page, but Wilberforce Montgomery had nothing more to say about the beetles, and was now busy hacking his way through a jungle in Malaya.

Today I traversed the Swamp by the Concealed path, carrying all my possessions as a cumbersome bundle upon my head. The water reached to my neck, and when I emerged, I was Delighted to find my naked body covered in Leeches, and small bloodsucking Fish of an unknown species. I collected several specimens.

Stella giggled. Wilberforce Montgomery continued through the swampy jungle, encountering tigers, vipers, stinging catfish, and other dangers. A drawing of a large, fleshy flower with a row of teeth around its center was spattered with greenish stains. Underneath was written: *Savage Corpse Lily.*

She read on. Wilberforce Montgomery climbed a volcano in the Sandwich Islands, investigating some strange lights that had been seen in the sky, and sat on the edge of the crater to toast some cheese. He paddled a birch-bark canoe up the Yukon River, on the trail of a hairy giant that had attacked a mining camp. He nearly drowned when the canoe capsized and sank in some rapids, and he was stranded on an island in the icy river for several weeks, eating snow and lichen and one of his own boots. He ventured into a pyramid in Egypt and discovered a passageway into a hidden tomb. *The doorway was hidden in a marvelously ingenious manner, and opened when I depressed both Eyes of the Carving, which depicted a coiled Serpent with two Heads.* There was a drawing of the carved serpent and the hidden levers and weights that unlocked the secret door.

"Stella! Stella! Where are you?"

She looked up, blinking. "I'm here," she called. She was startled to see that it was dusk outside. Night was approaching. She had not noticed the time passing at all.

From below came voices and the sounds of people stumbling around, and then Strideforth and Hortense climbed up into the room. Strideforth was carrying a candle. He grinned.

"Miss Araminter, she's up here!" he called.

Miss Araminter appeared on the stairs. She had cobwebs in her hair. She smiled at Stella. "There you are, my dear."

"It's the tower." Strideforth looked out of the

window. "You found the way up. You missed tea. Are you hungry? We've been looking all over the house for you. We thought you had disappeared. But then Hortense saw the bookcase had moved. It's hot up here, isn't it?" He touched the iron pipe that snaked along the wall and grinned with satisfaction. "There. I knew those pipes were going somewhere."

"I think this was Wilberforce Montgomery's study," said Stella.

"Look at all these things," said Strideforth. "How did you find the door? It was very well hidden."

"I heard buzzing." She showed him the empty cocoons. "There were insects trapped in here. They hatched because it's so warm, I think. They flew away into the garden. Look." Stella turned the pages of the journal, revealing the pictures of the lightning beetle, the savage corpse lily, and the hairy Yukon giant. "He was hunting for some very strange things. He brought some of them back with him. He had a secret collection."

"A secret collection?" Strideforth frowned and looked doubtfully at the drawings.

Miss Araminter was inspecting one of the dry seedpods that dangled overhead. She said, "My dears, I do believe this is a strangler vine from the Indies, and extremely rare. I know of only one specimen, in the Botanical Garden in Calcutta. It had to be confined within an iron cage after it garroted a gardener. A fascinating species. How unfortunate that it is dead." She gave the vine a pat. The dry leaves rustled.

Strideforth edged away from the tendrils of strangler vine. He put down the candle and tried on the pith helmet. It was much too large for him and came down over his ears. He picked up the telescope, wiped the lens with his sleeve, and peered through it. Hortense looked into the jars and tanks on the shelves. Anya squeaked at the bones of the snakebird creature.

Miss Araminter examined the shelves. "A mandragora root," she said. "And surely this is an assassin bean. Legendary and certainly extinct." She ran her fingers along the books. "*Carnivorous Seaweeds of the Sargasso. Malignant Wildflowers.* All four volumes. What a remarkable discovery, my dear," she said to Stella. "There are some treasures here." She looked around with a smile and rubbed her hands together. "It is almost dark. Tomorrow, when it is daylight, I will begin to make a proper inventory."

"It's suppertime," said Strideforth. "You must be hungry, Stella." He picked up the candle. Stella took a last glance around the study. Rain pattered against the windows, and outside, far below, the lake glinted in the last of the daylight. She shivered before following Strideforth down the stairs, clutching Wilberforce Montgomery's journal.

❧❦❧

That night, as Hortense slept, Stella sat up in bed and read more of the journal. The musical box sat beside her pillow, gleaming in the candlelight. Wilberforce Montgomery was traveling high in the mountains of Nepal, through a forest of enormous rhododendrons that was full of bandits and butterflies.

The locals talk of a Flying Serpent, but I have seen no trace of it, and today I was again bitten by many small Monkeys of an unknown species, and a Giant Hornbill of uncertain Temper.

There was a drawing of a huge bird with a high, arched bill. Its fierce, aristocratic expression and beady eyes reminded Stella of Aunt Deliverance. It was strange to think of the Aunts, so far away at the Hotel Majestic. It had been only two days since she had seen them, but already Stella felt as if they were part of a different world altogether.

She turned the page and followed Wilberforce Montgomery as he strode on through the rhododendron forest.

I have offered the Bandit Chief my Pocket Watch, several pairs of English woolen socks, and my last bottle of Finest Gentleman's Relish, in exchange for safe Passage through the high mountain pass.

Stella followed him up into the mountains, over glaciers, through snowstorms, and across perilous icy crevasses.

❧ ❦ ❧

Later she dreamed she was running through the rain, flitting silently along the hedgerows, trying to fade, to become invisible and hide. She could hear the men close behind, shouting to one another, boots thumping. Their lanterns were swinging in the darkness. She ran along the edge of the field, ducked through a thicket, slithered over a tumbledown fence, and slipped into the safety of the wood, as silent as a shadow.

Stella woke in darkness, gasping for breath, heart hammering. Raindrops pattered against the window. Henry snored. Outside, in the distance, an owl hooted. She thumped her damp, lumpy pillow into a more comfortable shape, turned over, and fell asleep again, clutching the musical box tightly against her chest.

⤳ Twelve ⤳

"Stella. Wake up!"

Stella opened her eyes and blinked in the gray morning light. Strideforth was shaking her arm. He was wearing the pith helmet from Wilberforce Montgomery's study while brandishing the telescope and the long butterfly net.

"What? Why?" She sat up and yawned.

"We were up in the tower. I looked out of the window. It's misty, but I think I saw that fish again. In the lake. We're going to see it. Perhaps we can catch it with this." He waved the butterfly net around, nearly hitting Hortense, who was standing behind him. Anya bristled and squeaked. Henry shrieked and flapped his wings.

Stella remembered the creature in the lake, with its wide black head and its rows of gleaming teeth. In *A Garden of Lilies*, Peregrine dipped his toe into the duck pond during his morning constitutional and was run over by a speeding velocipede.

> *One false step is all it takes,*
> *So keep away from ponds and lakes.*

Stella took a breath and clambered out of bed. "I'll get dressed," she said.

Strideforth grinned. "We'll wait for you downstairs."

Stella quickly pulled on two warm petticoats and her second-best dress. She twisted around with determination and managed to fasten almost all of the buttons. She tugged on a pair of warm woolen stockings and shoved her feet into her boots and laced them up.

She put Wilberforce Montgomery's journal with the tattered remains of *A Garden of Lilies*, underneath the heavy stone goldfish on the dressing table, where she hoped it would be safe from Henry. She touched the goldfish with her finger. It stared at her with cold stone eyes. She pushed the musical box under her pillow.

Strideforth and Hortense were waiting for her in the kitchen. Strideforth was jiggling from foot to foot and swinging the butterfly net around. "There you are," he said, knocking several books off the table. "Come on. Let's go."

Henry flapped his wings and shrieked, "*Eamus!*"

They pulled on their coats and went out into the drizzling rain. They hurried across the yard and made their way around the long row of empty stables, through the orchard, and across the terrace to reach the overgrown path that led to the lake. They climbed down the mossy steps, ducking under overhanging branches and pushing through the dripping, jungly garden. The lake, covered with water lilies, stretched away into mist.

"Shh," said Strideforth, mainly to Henry, who clicked his beak.

They went along slowly, following a path around the edge of the lake, through puddles and moss and tangles of wet ferns and palms and strange foreign plants. The waterfall trickled and splashed. Mist drifted. Somewhere in the garden, a peacock gave a mournful cry.

As they reached the arched stone bridge,

Strideforth said, "Perhaps it has gone—" Something splashed, and he stopped walking so suddenly that Stella bumped into him. He peered through the telescope. "I'm not sure. Just a frog, I think."

He passed the telescope to Stella. She leaned on the parapet of the bridge and looked through it. The water lilies glinted in the mist. A flash caught her eye.

"Look," she whispered. "It's one of the insects from the study. A lightning beetle."

They watched the beetle as it buzzed and sparked. It hovered above the water, then darted away and disappeared into the reeds farther along the bank. Stella passed the telescope to Hortense, who squinted through it with a frown, then shrugged and handed it back to Strideforth.

"Let's see if we can go all the way around the lake," said Strideforth.

Beyond the bridge, the path became even more overgrown and muddy. They pushed through prickly creepers and clambered over the trunks of fallen trees. A stone statue of a rabbit crouched beside the path. Stella hesitated.

"Come on," said Strideforth, shoving his way into the swampy undergrowth with determination.

Ahead, the summerhouse stood at the edge of the water. They splashed through muddy puddles,

ducked under the vines that trailed across the doorway, and went inside. It was a dark, damp little room.
There were walls on three sides. The side facing the
lake was open, with a balustrade and four ornate
stone columns, carved with Egyptian gods and
symbols.

Strideforth leaned on the balustrade and looked
out. "You can't see anything from here. The reeds are
too tall."

Stella hesitated. The air smelled of mildew. It was
oddly familiar. Something stirred at the back of her
mind. She saw four columns, dark shapes looming
up against a night sky. "I—I think I remember this,"
she said uncertainly.

Strideforth and Hortense turned around.

"It's in that painting," said Strideforth. "Wilberforce
Montgomery is sitting right here in the summerhouse. That's where you've seen it."

Stella shook her head. "No. I think I remember
being here before. When I was little."

The memory was faint, glimmering at the back of
her mind like a candle flame. The shape of the four
columns overhead. Fear. Hurry. Darkness. That was
all. She wanted to remember something more, but it
was like trying to catch hold of a wisp of smoke.

She looked around. The walls were streaked with

mold. Birds had built a straggling nest at the top of one of the columns. The floor was covered with mud and mounds of dead leaves.

Stella turned over some leaves with the toe of her boot. She saw something and bent to pick it up. It was a tiny wooden doll, the size of her longest finger. It wore the bedraggled remains of a dress that might have once been pink. It had jointed legs and arms and a few strands of wispy hair. It had been delicately carved, but it was rotten and worm-eaten, its painted face nearly worn away. Stella's fingers curved around the doll. It fitted into her hand, as if it belonged there.

Her throat felt tight. "I remember this," she whispered. "It was mine when I was little."

Hortense touched the doll timidly with her finger.

"You must have left it here," said Strideforth.

Stella stared at the doll's worn face. At the back of her mind, memory glimmered again. Lantern light, flickering. Someone was crying. Her mother was clasping her hand, pulling her along. She was very frightened, stumbling through the overgrown garden. Dark shapes loomed all around. She dropped her doll, but there was no time to stop and find it. And then she was going down and down, into darkness.

"I was here." Stella held her breath and clutched the little doll tightly, trying desperately to remember more. "It was dark. Nighttime. I was frightened," she said. "We had to hurry and be very quiet. Then we went down, into the dark." She sighed. What did it mean? Why had she been out in the garden at night? "That's all I can remember."

Strideforth opened his mouth to speak, but something splashed in the lake, and they all jumped.

"What was that?" Strideforth craned to see.

There was more splashing, out of sight.

Strideforth pulled off his boots and stockings and climbed up onto the balustrade. An overhanging tree grew close by. He clambered awkwardly up its trunk, carrying the telescope and the butterfly net, his feet slipping on the mossy bark. He scrambled out along a branch, high above the water, and balanced there, legs dangling.

Stella and Hortense peered through the reeds. They could see glimpses of the lake, dark and still.

Another lightning beetle darted past, glinting in the mist.

Strideforth wriggled farther along the branch and looked through the telescope. "I can see something," he whispered.

Henry gave a sudden shriek.

Strideforth twisted around with a frown. "Hush!" Then he squawked as he lost his balance and slipped sideways. His helmet fell off and splashed into the lake. The butterfly net fell and floated away. Strideforth clung onto the branch and tried to climb back up on top, but the bark was too slippery. He dropped the telescope, tried to catch it, lost his grip on the branch, yelled, waved his arms around, and then tumbled into the lake with a huge splash.

Stella and Hortense scrambled over the balustrade, jumped down into the reeds, and pushed their way through to the edge of the lake. Strideforth was splashing and floundering, tangled in the water lilies.

"Help!" he called, laughing and struggling. "I'm stuck."

Henry cackled rudely and flapped into the air. Stella and Hortense pulled off their boots and stockings. Stella pushed the little doll into the pocket of her coat. They tucked up their skirts and waded into the lake. The water was not as cold as Stella had expected, but it was unpleasantly murky and weedy. Her bare feet sank into the mud. Trailing strands of waterweed swirled and coiled around her legs as they waded deeper.

Something wriggled in the mud between her toes, and she squeaked. Hortense giggled.

They reached Strideforth. He was waist deep, and the water lilies were tangled around his arms and legs, tightening as he struggled. They tried to pull him free, but the stalks were too tough to break, as thick as ropes, slippery with slime and jagged with prickly spikes.

"Perhaps we can unwind them," said Stella.

Farther out, in the deep water, something moved. Stella caught her breath. Strideforth looked over his shoulder. A long, dark shape was swimming toward them.

Anya clambered up on top of Hortense's head, chittering anxiously.

Stella and Hortense tore desperately at the tangling stalks.

"Go!" shouted Strideforth, pushing them back toward the bank. "Don't wait for me."

Stella reached down underwater and wrapped her arm around the stalk of a water lily. She grasped it with both hands and heaved with all her strength. It snapped and she toppled backward. The green murky water closed over her head. She came to the surface, gasping for breath.

Strideforth said, "My knife!" He managed to pull it out from his pocket, but his wet hands slipped and fumbled and he nearly dropped it. Stella grabbed the knife and prized open a blade. She sawed through the tangled water lilies.

The creature swam closer. Its back arched as it dived.

"Here," said Strideforth. He took the knife and hacked through another stalk. He shoved the knife back into his pocket and fought his way free. He lost his balance and fell with a splash. Hortense and Stella seized his arms, hauled him to his feet, and pulled him toward the bank.

Stella felt the water move. She turned around.

The creature's wide black head came up out of the water, its gaping mouth bristling with thin, sharp teeth.

Hortense screamed.

Henry swooped down from the sky, shrieking. He flew past the creature's open jaws, flapped his wings, and swooped again.

They waded toward the bank as quickly as they could, struggling and splashing.

Behind them, Henry dived again, shrieking like a train whistle. The creature snapped its jaws and missed. Henry soared into the air, out of reach.

Stella stumbled over something. She fell and scrambled to her feet, gasping, clutching the heavy brass telescope. The creature appeared close behind them. Stella flung the telescope as hard as she could. It flew, end over end, missed the creature, and splashed into the water.

The creature lunged. Its teeth glinted.

Suddenly a lightning beetle flew out from the reeds, crackling with electricity. A cloud of beetles followed, sparking and buzzing. They surrounded the creature, darting and circling like streaks of light. The creature turned from side to side. Flashes of lightning snaked across the water. The creature gave a deep howl. It lurched and splashed. The beetles sparked still more. Lightning snapped and fizzed and crackled.

The water tingled and hissed. "Quick," gasped Stella. They floundered toward the bank.

The creature recoiled from the cloud of angry insects and dived underwater. The beetles swarmed above the surface, sparking and crackling. The creature surfaced and then dived again. The water swirled.

"It's going away," said Stella.

They reached the bank and shoved through the reeds and brambles, slipping and sliding in the mud. Panting, they clung together, watching the misty lake. Out in the deep water, the water lilies shifted. There were sparks and flashes of light. And then everything was still.

"It's gone," said Strideforth.

One of the lightning beetles darted back to them. It hovered in front of Stella's face for a moment, then flew around her, sending out tiny sparks, making her flinch and blink. It hovered again, making a high-pitched twittering sound, and then sped away.

Stella took a breath. Her wet hair was tingling, and the air smelled of burnt paper.

Henry flew down and landed on Hortense's head with a shriek. Anya hissed.

Strideforth coughed up some lake water. Stella and Hortense thumped him on the back. He spat out a bit of waterweed. "Well, we saw it, didn't we," he said, and grinned weakly.

✂✄ *Thirteen* ✂✄

*T*hey pulled on their stockings and boots, clambered over the balustrade into the summerhouse, and made their way back around the lake and up through the garden toward the house. Their sodden clothes clung to them and dripped. As they crossed the yard, a large owl swooped overhead.

Strideforth said, "Mrs. Burdock will be very angry, that is certain."

They pulled off their wet boots, left them in a row outside the back door, and crept inside in their stockings, leaving a trail of muddy water behind them. Mrs. Burdock met them halfway along the passageway with a shriek of horror and scolded them all the way up the stairs to their bedrooms. She shooed Henry away, dried their hair with a rough towel, and then stood over Stella and Hortense as they shivered and peeled off their wet clothes.

"I told you to keep right away from that lake," she snapped as she left the room with the dripping bundle.

Stella thought about the creature sliding through the dark water. She certainly did not want to go near the lake again. Not at all.

She sat the little battered doll on the dressing table beside the mirror. It stared at her as she pulled on clean drawers, a vest, and a petticoat. She tugged her third-best dress on over her head, twisted around, and managed to fasten all of the buttons.

She remembered clutching her mother's hand, hurrying through the darkness. What did it mean? She thought of the message on the tiny strip of paper: *Crossroads. Midnight. I will wait.* Had her mother been going to meet someone? But there were no crossroads in the garden.

The little doll stared back at her, without answers.

Stella picked up her hairbrush. Her reflection in the mirror looked pale. She noticed Hortense watching her again.

"Would you like me to brush your hair?" she offered.

Hortense shook her head.

Stella said, "Are you sure?"

Hortense hesitated for a moment, then shook her head again.

In the passage outside the kitchen, Mrs. Burdock was sweeping up muddy water with short, sharp strokes of her broom. Even her back looked cross. They tiptoed past her and found Miss Araminter sitting at the table in the kitchen, sipping a cup of tea. Beside her was a pile of books from Wilberforce Montgomery's study and several seedpods from the strangler vine. She had one of the volumes of *Malignant Wildflowers* propped open and was smiling to herself as she wrote things in her notebook. She looked up as they came in. "Good morning. You've been out early."

Mrs. Burdock poked her head around the door and said, "Firtling about in the lake. Wet as puddicks. Trailing slime and muck and who knows what into the house." She shook the broom at them. "If they were mine, ma'am, I'd learn them, I would."

"We're sorry, Mrs. Burdock," said Strideforth and Stella together.

"That's as may be."

Miss Araminter said vaguely, "You must

be more careful, my dears. The lake is rather deep."

"Catch their deaths, they will. Or drown. And serve them right, altogether," said Mrs. Burdock.

"I imagine they were admiring the *Victoria regia*. A fascinating specimen, you must agree, Mrs. Burdock. It is extraordinary for such a large water lily to be flowering outside the tropics. However, it is possible to observe it rather well from the bank, my dears. There is no necessity to immerse yourselves."

Mrs. Burdock looked exasperated. She shook her head and muttered something under her breath. Then she said, "And that dratted boy is late back with the bread and milk again. As much use as a cat in the custard, he is, the lazy scrogget." She rubbed her cheek. "The dentist's come, and I'm going to the village to get this aching tooth pulled. If I catch that boy firtling about there, I'll give him something to hurry him up, so I will."

"Please, Mrs. Burdock. Has the postman come today?" asked Strideforth.

"No, he has not," she snapped, and picked up the basket of washing and went away.

Strideforth pushed the end of the loaf of bread into the slicing machine and turned the handle. Henry shrieked. Everyone ducked. There was a clank and a whir, and several ragged pieces of bread were flung around the room. Strideforth collected them and spread them with jam.

"We saw something swimming in the lake," he said as he passed bread and jam to Stella and Hortense and opened a tin of sardines for Henry with his pocketknife. "Something big. I think it's a great big foreign fish."

Miss Araminter looked mildly surprised. "A foreign fish?"

Strideforth sat down at the table and nodded. "I think Wilberforce Montgomery must have brought it back from somewhere, years ago, and it's still here." He waved his arm toward the lake. "Swimming around down there. And growing bigger all the time."

"How very interesting," said Miss Araminter. "Did you get a close look at it?"

"Quite close," said Strideforth. He grinned at Stella and then took a big bite of bread and jam. "A bit too close, really."

❧

It was raining again. After lessons (botany, Latin, engineering, botany, mathematics, more botany, and then drawing) and dinner (bread and cheese and apples), Miss Araminter set them some preparation, wished them a pleasant afternoon, picked up her notebook, and hurried away to Wilberforce Mont-gomery's study. "I am going to examine the strangler vine," she said, smiling. "It will be a new chapter for my book."

Stella had a page of sums to complete, a list of Latin words to learn, and a diagram of a spider orchid to copy into her notebook. She had learned the Latin as well as she could and was about halfway through the sums when Anya shot out from Hortense's hair, twisting and jumping sideways and chittering. They heard piercing whistling out-side, and Jem peeked through the doorway.

He said, "Granny ain't here, is she? She'll clobber me if she sees me," and came in, dripping with rain. He put down the basket of bread and the can of milk. Anya dashed out at him, fur bristling. Jem laughed. "She's right savage, ain't she? Look what I got her." He took a piece of sausage from the pocket of his oilskin coat and held it out gingerly. Anya seized it and darted away. Jem grinned at her and rubbed his fingers together. "G'afternoon, Master Strideforth, Miss Hortense, Miss Stella."

Strideforth said, "We saw a big foreign fish in the lake this morning."

Jem grinned once more. "I heard you'd got all wet

through. Granny was carrying on something dreadful about it. She's right cross with you, she is." He laughed and rummaged in his pocket again, pulling out a piece of paper. "But look at this. The dentist's come. Mr. Flint. He pulled out Granny's tooth, just like he was cracking a nut. I seen it." He flattened the paper on the table. It was a printed notice.

Jethro Flint
DENTIST
Odditorium and Menagerie
Wax Statues of Noted Personages
Magic Lantern
Remarkable Curiosities!
Admission 1s, Children 6d.

Jem said, "He's put up his tent on the green. I want to go in, but I ain't got a tanner. And Granny says she ain't wasting good money on nonsense. So I've just been watching people go in and out. Seb Gromwell went in. He says there's all sorts in there. He says the waxworks were right creepy and gave him the shivers. He says there's a live chicken with two heads and a real mermaid."

"There's no such thing as mermaids," said Strideforth.

Jem shrugged. "Seb saw it. He says it's black and wrinkled, just lying there in a box. He says there's a 'Gyptian mummy too, which is a kind of dead foreign thing, wrapped up. Seb says the magic lantern's of a fire and a train wreck. He says it was right scary and some of the girls screamed. I'd like to see that, I would." He sighed wistfully.

Strideforth said, "I would too. I've never seen a magic lantern."

Jem lowered his voice. "Mr. Flint gave old Mrs. Crowfoot half a crown for a stone she found in her garden, what looks just like a toad. He says it's a curiosity and people will pay money to gawp at it. And he bought that huge great egg Mrs. Thorn's goose laid, for a shilling. So now Tom Pintucket and them want to catch the monster. Mr. Flint heard talk about it, that's why he come. He says he'll give them a sovereign for it, or even more, if they catch it or lead him to it. Depending."

"A sovereign!" said Strideforth.

"So he says. They went after it last night. I wanted to go too, but Granny wouldn't let me. They din't catch it, though. They din't even see it. Tom says they saw something pale flittin' along the road, and they chased it into Boggart Wood, but they were too frit to go in after it. Granny says it was likely just a hare."

Jem shrugged again. "If I got a sovereign, I'd go in the dentist's tent and see everything in there. And I'd get a toffee apple and an oyster pie, and a strawberry ice and a pair of white mice, and a whole pound of peppermints and a slingshot, I would. And I'd go and see the circus in Brockley. It comes in the summer, and I ain't never been. There are jugglers and clowns and all. And an elephant. Tom Pintucket says his cousin knows someone what saw it last time. Cobbin' great thing, he says. Big as a barn, with a hosepipe right there on his face." Jem waved his arm around in front of his nose. "Drank up thirteen bottles of porter, he did. And ate three dozen penny buns. It cost a shilling to see him. If I had a sovereign, I'd go all the way to Brockley on the train next summer and see the elephant ten times over."

He sighed again. "Anyway, I'm off afore Granny catches me. I'm meant to be picking slugs off the brussels sprouts. G'afternoon, Master Strideforth, Miss Stella, Miss Hortense." He put the loaf of bread on the table, picked up his basket, and hurried away. His boots clattered on the flagstones outside.

Stella jumped up and followed him out into the rain. "Jem, did you ask your grandmother about the lady who stayed here?"

Jem turned around and said awkwardly, "Well, I

asked her, Miss Stella. And she gave me a clip around the head."

"Oh, I am sorry," said Stella.

Jem rubbed his ear and grinned.

"Did she say anything at all?" she asked.

Jem hesitated, then said, "Well, she did say it's pure foolishness having children here, after what happened, and the house'd be far better left empty. And when I asked her what she meant by that, she gave me another clout and said I was as much use as a mole in the marmalade and to keep my nose out and my mouth shut, and come straight here and straight back, and don't linger about, gossiping. That's what she said."

"I'm sorry," said Stella again.

Jem grinned and shrugged, and went away around the side of the house, whistling.

Stella stood in the rain for a moment, thinking. She remembered what Ada had said at the railway station. She looked up at Wormwood Mire. It made a jagged shape against the dark rain clouds. What had happened here, all those years ago?

In the kitchen, Strideforth was reading the notice. "'Odditorium and Menagerie.' I'd like to see this, wouldn't you? We need sixpence each, though. Father gave us a half sovereign, but we spent most of it in

142

London. We don't have much left." He rummaged in his pockets, bringing out his pocketknife, a stub of a candle, a box of matches, a pencil, a curly piece of rusty wire, a ball of twine, some nails and screws and lumps of sealing wax, and several little coins. He counted them. "A groat, a penny, a ha'penny, and two farthings. This is only enough for one ticket."

"I've got a shilling," said Stella. "I was going to buy sweets."

"That's enough for two more tickets. Will we go if Miss Araminter says we may? It will be very interesting, that is certain."

Stella remembered another annoying story from *A Garden of Lilies*. Quentin watched a Punch-and-Judy show and later died of brain fever brought on by the excitement.

> *Misfortune always comes to those*
> *Who go to fairs and puppet shows.*

She frowned, nodded firmly, and said, "Yes, let's."

❧ Fourteen ❧

Miss Araminter said they might walk into the village. She reminded Stella to post the letter to the Aunts, saying, "They will be anxious to hear of your safe arrival, my dear," which Stella thought rather unlikely. They put on their coats and hats. Strideforth wound his long scarf around and around his neck. Anya perched on top of Hortense's hat like an elegant decoration. They left Henry behind in the kitchen with two tins of sardines, and they could hear his angry screams as they pulled on their boots in the yard.

"Last time he came with us to the village, he was very bad," said Strideforth. Hortense frowned at him, and he said, "Oh, you know he was, Hortense. He was very, very bad. He was enraged by the feathers on that lady's hat, so he snatched it right off her head and flew up to the top of the church tower and tore it to bits. Miss Araminter says now when we go to the village, he must stay at home."

Stella giggled, and Hortense gave a reluctant smile.

Mr. Burdock appeared with a wheelbarrow of coal.

"Good afternoon," said Strideforth. Mr. Burdock grunted something, trundled the wheelbarrow across the yard, and poured the coal down the chute that led to the furnace.

Stella pushed her foot into her boot and felt a scratch. "Ouch!" She turned the boot upside down and shook it. A little thorn fell out. It was black and curved and very sharp. She flicked it away, took off her stocking, and looked at her foot. There was a scratch and a bead of blood, no bigger than the head of a pin. She wiped it away, pulled her stocking back on, put on her boot, and laced it up.

Strideforth said, "Are you ready? Let's go."

They followed the drive around to the front of the house.

"Which is the nursery?" Stella asked Strideforth.

"That window there, at the end."

Stella walked backward up the drive, looking at the window of the nursery. She thought of her mother crying in the rocking chair, watching and waiting.

"It's so strange to think of her here. Who was she waiting for? And what was she doing, at night, down in the summerhouse by the lake? I think she was going to meet someone."

"It is very strange, really," said Strideforth.

"And nobody will tell me anything. My Aunts would never answer my questions. Mrs. Burdock wouldn't say, and Jem asked her, and she wouldn't tell him, either. But I think she knows something."

"What happened, do you think?" asked Strideforth.

"Something dreadful." Stella gazed up at the window. "But even so, I do want to know."

"You remembered some things," said Strideforth. "Perhaps you will remember more, if you try."

Mrs. Burdock was hanging up washing outside the gatehouse, frowning at Jem, who was crouched nearby in the little vegetable garden, weeding diligently. He looked up and grinned at them, but did not stop work.

Mrs. Burdock said, "Off to the village, are you?" She stomped off into the gatehouse and came back with a large key. She unlocked the huge, curly iron gate and pulled it open. "Stay on the road. And mind you're back before dark."

The gate creaked and clanged as Mrs. Burdock

shut it behind them and turned the key in the lock. They walked along a muddy lane, winding between high banks and overgrown hedgerows. An icy wind blew across the fields, and Stella pushed her hands into the pockets of her coat.

"That is Boggart Wood," said Strideforth as they crossed a bridge. He pointed down the hill toward a dense tangle of trees, a dark shape in the valley below. They went on, past scattered farms and clumps of wintry trees and swampy thickets and sheep. A flock of jackdaws croaked and tumbled in the blustery wind. A gray horse stood looking over a hedge. Hortense stopped and patted its nose and whispered something into its ear.

"There's the church," said Strideforth. "You can see the tower above the trees."

As they reached the edge of the village, they could hear clanking, wheezing music playing. They walked down the street. A small, shabby circus tent stood on the muddy grass beside the inn. Strings of wet flags flapped in the breeze. Stella posted her letter in the pillar box outside the post office. She stopped and looked down the alleyway toward the sweetshop. Something pale flickered in the window.

"Come on," said Strideforth.

Stella hesitated for a second, then followed

Strideforth and Hortense across the green to join the crowd that had gathered outside the tent.

A gangling youth with a gormless expression and a number of missing teeth was turning the handle of the barrel organ. Women carrying baskets and bundles were standing around, gossiping, and a group of young men was lounging against the wall of the inn. Shopkeepers stood on their steps, arms folded. Children were running and laughing and shouting.

Above the entrance to the tent was a peeling sign, painted red and gold. On one side was a picture of a fat mermaid with a long, gleaming tail. She was holding a mirror and simpering at her reflection. On the other side was a two-headed rooster. Both of its heads were crowing. Between the pictures was written, in fancy gold letters:

Jethro Flint
DENTIST
Odditorium and Menagerie

The flaps of painted canvas at the entrance to the tent parted, and a man emerged. "Step up, step up," he said with a bow. He was small and wiry, not much taller than Stella herself, and he wore a tall hat and a velvet tailcoat, decorated with tarnished sequins and gilt thread. His eyes were wide set and as green as gooseberries. A jagged row of extracted teeth was sewn around his hatband. His gaze darted over the crowd, alert and watchful. "Jethro Flint, dentist. A toothache? A niggle? A little gripe? Fix you right up. Quick as a winking. Gone before you know it. No time to yell. You'll be chomping up bones and gristle this very night, just like a lord."

A laughing group pushed a reluctant young man forward. His face was pale and his cheek was swollen.

"Step up. This way, cully, this way." Mr. Flint placed a wooden chair on the grass in front of the tent and shoved the pale young man into it. He tilted the man's head back. "Now, open your potato trap, and let's get a look at these here dinner manglers." He pulled the man's mouth open and prodded around inside with his fingers. "This one? Yes? This one here?"

The man made a muffled reply.

"Half a crown, cully."

The man handed him a coin. Mr. Flint took it, bit it, and put it in his pocket. He produced a tool that looked rather like a long pair of pliers. He called to the youth at the barrel organ, "Give it some pepper, lad." The youth's vacant expression did not change, but he turned the handle faster and the music jolted along more quickly.

The crowd murmured and moved closer. People jostled one another and stood on tiptoe to see.

Again, Mr. Flint pushed the man's head back and pulled his jaw open. "Hold hard," he said, and reached into the man's mouth with the pliers.

The clanking music sped up a bit more.

Stella shut her eyes.

The crowd breathed in.

There was a horrible little crack.

The crowd gasped, and then broke into applause. Stella opened her eyes. Mr. Flint held up a tooth, gripped in the jaws of the pliers. The pale young man looked even paler than before. He had blood on his chin. He fumbled for his handkerchief and pressed it to his mouth.

Mr. Flint dropped the tooth into his waistcoat pocket, tucked the pliers away, pulled the young man upright, and patted him on the back. "Well done, cully." The crowd clapped again. Mr. Flint bowed and said, "Step up, step up. Flint's wondrous odditorium and menagerie. Tantalize your senses. Amaze your intellect."

A few people pushed forward. Coins clinked. Mr. Flint passed them little paper tickets, pulled back the canvas at the entrance to the tent, and waved them inside.

Strideforth dug in his pocket for the coins. "Will we go in?" he asked.

Stella hesitated, Hortense took a step backward, and Anya hissed. They watched several more people go into the tent, venturing cautiously into the darkness.

Strideforth took a breath. "Come on," he said.

As she followed Strideforth through the crowd, Stella thought she heard whispering and turned around. A cluster of women were talking in low voices. One of them met Stella's gaze and quickly looked away.

Mr. Flint bowed, his gleaming green eyes fixed on Stella. "Good afternoon to you, young ladies, young gentleman," he said. "Sixpence apiece."

On Hortense's hat, Anya chittered angrily at him, her fur spiky.

"Look there. A little white whitterick," Mr. Flint

said. "I'll give you half a crown for it, cully. A nice curiosity, that. Stuffed and mounted, like." He fished in his pocket and pulled out a handful of coins and several teeth.

Hortense hissed at him, scowling. She snatched Anya off her hat and held her tight against her front.

Mr. Flint laughed and dropped the coins and teeth back into his pocket. "No? Well, you won't get a better offer."

Strideforth counted one and six into his hand. Mr. Flint pocketed the coins so quickly it was like a vanishing trick, and gave them a ticket each. "Step inside, step inside. Wonders and marvels. Astound your reason. Curdle your entrails."

He pulled back the curtains and bowed.

Fifteen

*I*t was dark inside the tent, and it smelled of mold and mothballs and wet sawdust. Mirrors and silvery paint glinted. They followed a canvas passage around, before stopping with a gasp.

Three huge pale figures with enormous wobbling heads loomed up in front of them.

After a second, Strideforth said, "It's just a mirror."

The curved surface of the mirror made Stella's reflection as long and bony as Aunt Temperance, and then as short and round as Aunt Condolence. The children bobbed up and down and giggled to see themselves stretch and shrink.

They went on and came to a group of wax figures. There was Florence Nightingale (in a dark dress and a white lace cap, holding a lantern), Dr. Livingstone (with a thick, bristling mustache that looked as if it were made from a clothes brush and an unconvincing palm tree) and the Duke of Wellington (looking dashing and noble in a red coat with a bright-blue sash). Stella eyed them nervously. They had vivid, flushed cheeks and leaned stiffly at awkward angles. Dr. Livingstone was missing an arm, and the Duke of Wellington looked particularly unstable, propped up from behind with a broomstick. Their glass eyes glistened in the wavering lantern light and seemed to follow her as she edged past.

Beyond the waxworks was a crowded display of curiosities. Several people were peering into a wooden case with a glass lid. A sign read THE FEEJEE MERMAID. Inside the case was a twisted shape no larger than a baby. It had a head and arms, but where its legs should have been was a scaly tail. It was impossible to see any of its features; it was as black and shriveled as a prune.

"It is sewn together," said Strideforth, his face almost touching the glass. "It's half a monkey, I think, and half a fish. There are stitches. Look."

Stella looked and nodded, and then looked away again quickly.

Nearby was a mossy rock shaped like a crouching toad. The sign read

TOADSTONE. A large bluish egg was labeled MONSTROUS EGG. CURIOSITY OF NATURE. Next, a small creature, perhaps a cat, was covered in tightly wound grimy bandages. Little tufts of ginger fur poked out. It had a sweetish, sickly smell. The sign read ANCIENT EGYPTIAN MUMMY. AUTHENTIC AND GENUINE. Anya darted out to attack it. Hortense grabbed her and held her firmly as she wriggled and squeaked.

"Here's the two-headed chicken," said Strideforth. A few people were clustered around a cage, poking at a small creature that huddled inside. The chicken looked very dejected. Its four eyes were closed. Some of its feathers were missing, and its skin was as pale as milk. Hortense clucked at it, and it lifted one of its heads listlessly and made a sad little croak.

A light flickered. People were packed into an alcove where another young man with dull eyes and several missing teeth was operating the magic lantern, shining the images onto the canvas wall of the tent. The magic lantern looked like a little tin temple. It emitted clicks and hisses and a strong smell of scorched metal. The young man pushed the glass slides into it, one at a time, and jiggled the levers to make the images move.

"Come on," said Strideforth. He pulled Hortense away from the sad chicken, and they squeezed their way in. The light flickered. A ship rose and fell on the waves of a stormy sea. A lady's head changed into the head of a dog, then a skull, then a monster. A man chased a butterfly and caught it in his hat. Two children rode on a seesaw, up and down. Three blackbirds broke out of a pie and flew away.

Click, click, click. The scenes followed one another. A train crossed a canyon, smoke puffing from its funnel, and then teetered and fell from the bridge. Some of the audience gasped. A red fire consumed a building. Someone screamed. Stella stood on tiptoe to see, but taller people crowded in around her, blocking her view with their arms and backs, smelling of wet wool and vegetables. In the darkness, she lost sight of Strideforth and Hortense. She was bumped and shoved and nearly lost her balance. Someone trod heavily on her foot, and she squeaked at the sudden stabbing pain, but her voice was lost amongst the shrieks of the audience.

Click, click, click. The light flickered, yellow and orange and red. There were more gasps and screams.

Stella struggled back through the crowd. She

took a breath, looked around, saw daylight filtering in, and heard the barrel organ. She limped toward the entrance, pushed aside the canvas curtains, and hobbled outside.

It was drizzling. Stella spied a wooden crate beside the dentist's wagon, and she went over and sat down on it. She unlaced her boot, pulled off her stocking, and inspected her foot. It was red and bruised and painful. She leaned back against the wagon and rubbed her foot as she waited for Strideforth and Hortense to come out of the tent.

People were milling around, talking and laughing. The strings of flags flapped and dripped and the music from the barrel organ clanked and wheezed.

Mr. Flint stood nearby, surrounded by a group of children. He beckoned them closer and flipped open his coat. "Buy a top? Buy a whistle? Threepence, fourpence apiece," he said. Attached to the lining of his coat were several rows of painted wooden tops and shiny tin whistles.

Out of the corner of her eye, Stella saw something hovering at the edge of the group of children. When she looked at it directly, it disappeared. A few moments later, she saw it again, but it vanished as she turned her head.

It happened so quickly that she had almost

convinced herself that she had imagined it when she saw it a third time, moving toward her through the crowd. It shimmered at the edge of her vision, about the size of a child, as pale as smoke and almost invisible. Nobody else seemed to notice it as it drifted closer to where she was sitting and hovered, several yards away, almost as if it were watching her. Then it turned and sped away across the green.

Stella pulled on her stocking and shoved her foot into her boot without stopping to lace it up. She limped after the pale shape as quickly as she could. It darted away from her toward the shops. It was difficult to follow, wavering and shifting like breath on a cold morning. Several times it vanished altogether and appeared again, farther along the street. Stella hobbled after it, past the forge and the post office, stumbling over the cobblestones. Outside the grocer's, she lost sight of it. She leaned against a lamppost to catch her breath and looked up and down the street.

Somewhere, a bell jangled.

Stella recognized the sound. She hobbled past the ironmonger's and reached the alleyway just in time to see the door of the sweetshop close.

Cautiously she crept along the alley and peered in through the rippled glass of the window.

Something moved.

A face swam into sight behind the sweet jars. A pale face with wide, startled eyes. Stella gasped before she realized it was her own reflection, distorted by the rippled glass and the greenish flickering light. She put her hand on the window, and on the other side of the glass, her reflection reached toward her.

Suddenly an angry voice came from inside the shop. An old woman's voice. Stella jumped back from the window. Her reflection disappeared.

"Where've you been? Outside, flitting about? Stay hid, Tick. I told you. Stay inside. Stay hid." A small voice answered and the old woman snapped, "None of that." The door handle rattled and the bell jangled again as the door was flung open.

Frightened, Stella took two steps away from the window, but there was no time to run. She wanted to hide. She felt herself begin to fade. Her head swam as she dissolved into shadow and disappeared.

Mrs. Spindleweed stood on the step, glaring. "Who's there? Creeping around. Spying and prying. I know you're there. Who is it? Who?"

Invisible, Stella stood as still as a stone, her heart beating in her ears.

Mrs. Spindleweed tilted her head, listening. Her strange yellow eyes scanned the alleyway. Stella held her breath. For a moment, she was sure Mrs. Spindleweed had seen her. Then there was a clattering noise upstairs in the sweetshop. Mrs. Spindleweed blinked and muttered something to herself. She went back into the shop, slamming the door. Footsteps clumped up the stairs. After a minute, an owl hooted overhead.

Stella took a deep breath, turned away, and limped back along the alley to the street as quickly as she could. She felt herself begin to appear again. It was a dizzying, prickling sensation. She shivered and pushed her hands into the pockets of her coat.

As she turned into the street, a figure stepped out in front of her. Stella gasped. It was Mr. Flint, the dentist. She stumbled and nearly fell. His hand darted out and caught her arm.

"Careful there, cully," he said.

"I'm sorry," she said.

"Don't you fret, young lady. Don't you fret." His fingers tightened on her arm. His green eyes glittered. "You're all of a fluster. What frightened you?"

"N-nothing," she stammered. Had he been

watching her? Had he seen her disappear?

"Shaking like a leaf, you are." He smiled. His gaze was very alert. "What did you see? Something fearsome?"

"No. It was nothing." She looked over her shoulder. The alley was empty. She said, "An owl. It was just an owl."

"A hoolet." Mr. Flint nodded. "Such as might startle anyone on a dark afternoon, if come across unexpected-like." He pulled her closer. His breath smelled of cloves and tobacco. "Now, cully. I've been hearing whispers and rumors from hereabouts. A monster of some description. I'm after getting my grabblers on it. A nice curiosity, that would make. Very nice indeed. What do you know about that?"

Stella said, "I don't know anything."

"No? Well, if you clap your peepers on it, you tip me the wink. I'll make it worth your while, cully. My word on it." Stella tried to pull away from his grasp. He smiled, and his fingers tightened on her arm once more. "Now, don't go dashing away like that. How are your teeth? Any little aches? Any little niggles?" He pulled the long pair of pliers from his pocket and snapped its jaws. *Click, click.*

Stella shook her head.

"Quick as a wink. You won't even know it's gone.

I give you my word." He snapped the pliers again. *Click, click.*

"N-no," stammered Stella.

"You won't feel a thing. Not a snicket."

"No." She pulled her arm free. "No. I'm sorry. I—I have to go."

Mr. Flint gave her a bow, without taking his eyes from her face. "Well, good afternoon to you, then, young lady." He slipped the pliers back into his pocket.

Stella hurried away along the street. She looked behind for a moment. He was watching her. The teeth around his hat gleamed. She saw him take something small and white from his waistcoat pocket and push it into his ear.

ᴄᴡᴏ Sixteen ᴄᴡᴏ

Strideforth and Hortense were waiting beside
the tent, sheltering under a tree.

"There you are," said Strideforth. "Where did you
go? We thought you were lost. You're limping. What
happened?"

"Someone stood on my foot in the dark," said
Stella. "And I saw—I don't know what I saw." She
remembered Jem saying Mrs. Spindleweed had an
invisible thing in the sweetshop to run errands for
her. A familiar. Had the wispy, invisible shape been
a familiar? It seemed very unlikely. And she was not
going to tell Strideforth that she might have seen a
familiar. She knew what he would think about that.
"I bumped into Mr. Flint," she said. "He was talking
about the monster. He wants to catch it."

"There's no such thing, that is certain," said

Strideforth. "Is your foot all right? Does it hurt?"

"Only a bit." She crouched to tie her bootlace. Her fingers were trembling.

"Did you see the magic lantern? Did you see the train wreck? And the fire? We watched it three times through. A girl fainted dead away and they carried her outside. It was very interesting." He sighed happily. "Are you sure you're all right? You look—"

Stella stood up and took a breath. She said, "Yes. Yes. I'm quite well."

"It will be dark soon," said Strideforth. He squinted up at the sky. "And it's raining. We should go. Can you walk, do you think?"

They went along the street. People hurried past, muffled in their coats, heads bent against the rain. Some of the shopkeepers had lit their lamps, and others were already putting up their shutters.

The rain was becoming heavier. Gray clouds were piling up overhead. As they left the village, there was a rumble of thunder. Stella hugged her coat around herself and hobbled on as well as she could, slipping and stumbling. She stopped to catch her breath and glanced back. A faint light glimmered in the window of a farmhouse, and on the lane behind, a distant figure was hurrying home before dark.

Stella limped on, shivering in the cold rain. The

trees in the hedgerows creaked in the wind. In the dusk, Boggart Wood was no more than an indistinct shadow. She felt the back of her neck prickle, looked behind, and saw the figure again. She stopped and shielded her eyes, but in the rain and the fading light, she could see only a pale, flickering shape.

"Who is that?" she asked.

Strideforth turned around. "There is nobody," he said.

Hortense looked and shrugged and shook her head.

Stella blinked. The figure had gone.

She saw something move, but it was just an owl swooping silently across the fields.

They went on.

Stella looked back over her shoulder several times, but the lane behind remained empty.

❧

By the time they reached Wormwood Mire, the rain was pelting down. Stella was cold and shivering, and her bruised foot hurt with a sharp, stabbing pain. Mrs. Burdock was watching for them. She came out of the gatehouse and unlocked the tall iron gate. "What time do you call this?" she said, frowning as she followed them down the drive.

165

"We're sorry, Mrs. Burdock," said Strideforth and Stella together.

"As much use as jackdaws in the junket, you are. I've got better things to do than come out in the wet like this. Did you see that boy in the village?"

"Jem? No," said Strideforth.

"Where's he got to, then? He'll be slummocking about, the lazy lump. I'll knock some sense into his head when he turns up, I will." She glared at them. "Get yourselves safe inside, now. It's near on dark." She turned and stomped back to close the gate.

"Poor Jem," said Stella as they hurried down the drive toward the house.

In the kitchen, the lamps were lit, the heating pipes hissed, and a bright fire crackled in the range. Henry flapped over from the mantelpiece and landed on Hortense's head. He shrieked several Latin words into her face, making her giggle.

Miss Araminter sat at the table. She had cut open a pod from the strangler vine and extracted some seeds, as shiny and black as ebony beads. She was examining them through a microscope. She looked up and smiled vaguely at them. "Good evening, my dears. Did you have a pleasant afternoon?"

"We saw the magic lantern," said Strideforth as they took off their dripping coats and hats and hung them up. "And an Egyptian mummy and a two-headed chicken, and a mermaid, but that was not real, I think. We saw the dentist pull out a tooth. It was very interesting. But Stella's foot is hurt. Somebody stepped on it."

"Oh, how unfortunate. Let me see." Miss Araminter propelled Stella into a comfortable armchair beside the range, gently took off her boot and stocking, and inspected her foot. "A rather nasty bruise, I'm afraid, my dear." She wrapped her own shawl around Stella's shoulders and gave her a pat. "Stay there." She lit the lantern and pulled on her cape and hat. "It is rather cold this evening. Strideforth, perhaps you would make cocoa for supper? I will return directly." She picked up her umbrella and went out into the garden.

Strideforth filled a saucepan with milk and put it on the range. He pushed the bread into the slicing machine and made a pile of raggedy jam sandwiches. He opened a tin of mackerel for Henry.

"Does it hurt?" he asked Stella as he passed her a cup of hot cocoa and a sandwich.

"Thank you." She took a sip of cocoa, and then poked her bruised foot with her finger. "A bit."

They were finishing their supper when Miss Araminter returned. "Henbane, comfrey, and wormwood," she said, striding into the kitchen with a bundle of dripping plants under her arm. "Marvelous for inflammation. And look, my dear—Brazilian fever tree." She brandished a long, trailing stem with several fleshy, yellowish leaves. "It will be rather interesting to see its effect, don't you agree?"

Stella nodded doubtfully.

"Splendid," said Miss Araminter. "I will make a poultice." She chopped up the plants and put them in a pot of water on the range. When it boiled, filling the kitchen with a strong-smelling steam, she mixed it into a green paste, added some oil from the tin of mackerel, and spread it onto Stella's injured foot. It was warm and smelled of wet gardens and fish. Miss Araminter wrapped a clean handkerchief around it as a bandage. "There." She pinned it neatly in place and gave Stella's foot a pat.

"Thank you," said Stella.

Miss Araminter smiled as she wrote something in her notebook. "An early night for you, then, my dear." She helped her up. "Do you need assistance getting upstairs? Does it hurt at all?"

Stella wriggled her toes. "It feels a bit better," she said.

"Marvelous," said Miss Araminter, and made another note. "It should be as good as new in the morning."

Stella took a candle and said good night. She used the lavatory quickly. The wet, mossy walls glinted in the candlelight. She pulled the chain and jumped away from the splashing water. As she limped along the dark passage toward the stairs, an icy gust made her shiver. Outside, rain pelted down. The wind sent something clattering across the yard.

Ahead, a pale shape seemed to scamper up the narrow stairs that led to the bedrooms.

"Strideforth?" Stella called. There was no answer. She peered up into the darkness. The wavering candlelight made the shadows flicker. She climbed the stairs cautiously. As she reached the top, there was a flash of lightning, and she thought she saw something dart into a room at the end of the winding passage.

"Who's there?" she asked, her voice faltering.

She tiptoed along the passage to the room at the end. The door was closed. She hesitated, her trembling fingers on the door handle, heart hammering. Thunder rumbled.

"Come on," she whispered to Letty, and took a breath and pushed the door open.

It was an empty bedroom. Whitewashed walls, a rusty bed frame, and a broken chair. She looked behind the door and under the bed. Nothing but cobwebs and dust.

Stella let out a shaky breath. She was imagining things in the shadows. Of course old houses were full of drafts and creaks and other strange noises. No need to be so nervous.

She closed the door and went back along the passage to her own bedroom. The window had blown open and the rain was coming in. Outside, an owl hooted. Stella closed the window, pushed the latch across, and drew the curtains, shutting out the dark. She wound up the musical box and opened the lid. Humming along to the tinkling, whispering tune, she propped the little photograph against the mirror. The three tiny faces stared at her, wide-eyed. She patted the little doll with her finger, then opened Wilberforce Montgomery's diary so she could read it as she got ready for bed. He was in Madagascar, traveling through forests full of bottle-shaped trees, meeting lemurs and chameleons and other strange creatures. *While picnicking on the mountainside, I encountered an Elephant Bird, full ten feet tall. It purloined my Sandwich, and made off into the forest with Raucous Cries.*

Stella changed into her nightgown, picked up her hairbrush, undid her hair, and began to brush it. Something scratched her forehead. It was a sharp pain, like the prick of a needle. A little thorn was stuck in amongst the bristles of the brush. She picked it out carefully and examined it in the light of the candle. It was like the one she had found in her boot, curved like the claw of a bird, black and needle-sharp.

She inspected her forehead in the mirror and saw a tiny scratch above her eye and a speck of blood.

The candle flame flickered, and Stella felt a cold breath of air on the back of her neck. The bedroom door was ajar. She went over and closed it.

She sat down at the dressing table, turned the page in Wilberforce Montgomery's journal, and read on as she brushed her hair. He was investigating some caves. *The Natives believe they conceal a Creature of considerable size. I am determined to encounter it.* She began to plait her hair as Wilberforce Montgomery squeezed down narrow tunnels and swam across underground rivers and ventured into huge caverns.

Behind her reflection in the mirror, something moved.

Stella froze and held her breath.

For a moment, nothing happened. Then the door handle turned silently, and the door swung slowly open.

⁓ Seventeen ⁓

Stella spun around. "Strideforth? Is that you?" There was no answer.

She hesitated, then picked up the candle and tiptoed toward the open door. The passageway outside was empty, winding away into darkness.

"Who's there? Strideforth? Hortense?" She tried to stop her voice from shaking.

She held her breath, listening to the rain and the wind and the tinkling tune from the musical box.

A floorboard creaked.

Stella jumped. The candle flared, making the shadows lurch.

Another creak. As if someone were creeping toward her.

There was a gust of icy air, and the candle sputtered and went out.

Stella stumbled back across the bedroom to the dressing table and groped around in the darkness for the matchbox. She opened the box, her fingers fumbling. She tried to strike a match.

Behind her came the sound of a soft footstep, and then another. Something brushed against her. She shrieked. The matches scattered and the candle rolled away across the floor.

"Who's there?" Her voice was a croak.

The musical box slowed, and ran down, and stopped.

There was a sharp smell, somehow familiar.

Suddenly, out of the darkness, a hand gripped hers. Cold, clutching fingers. Wispy, like smoke.

Lightning flashed, and Stella had a glimpse of a white face with wide, frightened eyes. She gasped and staggered backward.

A clap of thunder made the window rattle. Something clattered against the roof. An owl hooted. She heard a quick indrawn breath, and the clutching hand disappeared. Footsteps fled along the passage.

Stella felt her way toward the door. Her hands groped only empty air. Then her head collided with something hard. She clasped her forehead and saw stars, flashing and swirling around in dizzying circles, and dissolving into nothing.

"Stella. My dear. Whatever has happened?"

Stella opened her eyes. Lantern light glimmered. She was lying on the floor of the bedroom. She sat up, shivering and dizzy.

"There was something— There was someone here, in the dark—"

"It's only us," said Strideforth. "Did you fall?" He picked up the scattered matches and lit the candle.

"You fainted. You hit your head on the door," said Miss Araminter. She touched Stella's forehead gently. "Does it hurt?" She helped Stella up and half carried her over to her bed. "Lie down, my dear." She pulled up the bedcovers. "There. You are shivering." She rubbed Stella's hands between her own.

Hortense perched on the edge of Stella's bed, looking anxious. Anya peered out from behind her neck and chittered.

"There was someone here," Stella said.

"You had a fright," said Miss Araminter, patting her. "You're dazed, and no wonder."

"The door opened. The lightning flashed, and I saw a face," said Stella.

Strideforth said, "There is nobody here except us."

He looked under the bed and inside the wardrobe.

He went along the passageway, in and out of the other bedrooms. Stella could hear him banging around. He came back and said, "Probably it was just the wind blowing open the door. And you got confused in the dark, which can happen very easily. And you saw your own face in the mirror. That was all."

Stella's forehead ached. It was a sharp, stabbing pain. "I don't know—" She remembered the startled, wide-eyed face she had seen in the flash of lightning. Had it been her own reflection?

And the ghostly, clutching hand. Had she imagined it?

"Close your eyes, my dear," said Miss Araminter. "You will feel much better in the morning." She patted Stella again. "I will bring something for your head and make you some hot milk with dandelion and poppy." She picked up the lantern and went away.

"Does it hurt?" asked Strideforth.

"A bit." Stella touched her forehead and winced.

She remembered the sharp, familiar scent. Where had she smelled it before? "Peppermint," she said. "Peppermint and licorice."

"What?"

"Peppermint and licorice." She sat up. "From the sweetshop."

"What do you mean?" asked Strideforth.

177

"That's what I smelled, here in the room. Jem said that Mrs. Spindleweed has an invisible thing that runs errands for her," said Stella. "A familiar."

"There's no such thing as a familiar, that is certain," said Strideforth. He sniffed the air, frowning. "Jem should not believe things like that."

"I saw it in the village, too. It was an invisible shape. It must have followed us here."

"How could you see an invisible shape? That does not make sense," said Strideforth. "And why would it follow us? If it even exists, which it does not. Perhaps you were dreaming. Dreams can seem very real sometimes."

Stella hesitated. Could she have dreamed it? Recently her dreams had been very strange and vivid. She rubbed her forehead.

"No," she said uncertainly. "I'm sure there was something here."

⁂

Stella slept heavily and dreamed she was hiding in a tangled shrubbery. Cold rain pelted down. There were men nearby. She could hear them and see the flickering light from their lanterns. A dog whined.

She ducked down and made herself fade, disappearing into the darkness. She barely noticed the cold or felt the scratches of the twigs and thorns. She heard an owl hoot and crouched as still as a stone, silent and invisible as it swooped past. Then she crept out of her hiding place and ran through the wild rain and the dark. She sang to herself as she ran, a whispering, melancholy tune, like raindrops falling on leaves.

⚜

Stella was jolted awake by a crashing, jangling clang. Hortense gave a little shriek and Henry screamed. Stella sat up in bed and stared into the darkness, her heart hammering.

The bedroom door banged open and Strideforth bounded into the room, grinning. "It's the doorbell. It worked very well, didn't it? It's very loud."

"It is," agreed Miss Araminter, behind him. She carried a candelabra and wore a woolen dressing gown with a cheerful tartan pattern. "Very loud indeed. Whoever could be calling so late? And in such dreadful weather?"

The doorbell clanged again.

179

"How is your head, my dear?" asked Miss Araminter.

"It feels much better," said Stella. She scrambled to her feet before Miss Araminter could tell her to stay in bed. Shivering, she and Hortense wrapped themselves in the velvet curtains from their beds. Stella pushed her feet into her slippers. Miss Araminter led them along the passage and down the stairs. The night was full of moans and creaks and rattles and drips. The candle flames reflected on the glass cases, and their shadows made huge swooping shapes. Henry flew ahead into the darkness, shrieking. The doorbell rang again, sending jangling echoes through the house. They reached the entrance hall. Someone was hammering on the front door. A dog barked.

"Who is there?" called Miss Araminter.

"It's me, ma'am. Mrs. Burdock."

Miss Araminter passed Strideforth the candelabra, pulled back the bolts, and opened the door.

Mrs. Burdock stood on the threshold, wrapped in a woolen shawl, dripping with rain. Behind her was a group of wet men. They had long sticks and lanterns and several dogs on leads. They gasped and ducked as Henry flew out over their heads and flapped off into the garden.

Miss Araminter said, "Mrs. Burdock. Whatever

is the matter? Do come in out of the rain."

Mrs. Burdock's face was white in the lantern light. She said, "I am sorry to disturb you so late like this, ma'am." She pressed her hand to her forehead. "It's the boy, Jem. He din't come home."

Stella gasped. "Oh no."

"He's not here then, ma'am, by any chance?"

"No, I'm very sorry, he is not."

"Where's he got to, then? Fooling about, no doubt. When he turns up, I'll wallop him, I will." Her voice faltered. "Where has he gone? Did he say anything to you children?"

They looked at one another and shook their heads.

"Nothing at all?"

Strideforth said, "He did say he wanted to go and see the dentist's tent."

One of the men cleared his throat. "He weren't there. Nobody saw him go in."

Mrs. Burdock said, "He knows I won't have him wasting good money on foolishness."

Stella caught Strideforth's glance. She hesitated. "He said— He was talking about the monster."

The men exchanged glances, and one of them looked nervously over his shoulder, out at the rainy dark.

Mrs. Burdock frowned. "All this talk about the

monster is just nonsense, Miss Stella," she said. "Silly nonsense."

"But—"

"No. Jem ain't foolish. He knows better than that."

Miss Araminter said, "Come in out of the rain, won't you? Can we offer you hot drinks? Or sandwiches?"

One of the men said, "No thank you, ma'am. We'll search the garden here, with your permission. Then we'll be heading out to Dodder Wake and back past Yarrow, along by the canal."

Mrs. Burdock said, "There's search parties going out all over. Mr. Burdock's gone out with them, toward Spurge Farm and around through Horsetail Wood. I must get back home, in case—" She put a shaking hand to her mouth.

Miss Araminter said, "No doubt he has taken shelter somewhere, in this dreadful weather. I'm sure you will find him safe."

Mrs. Burdock's voice quivered. "I truly hope so, ma'am," she said.

"I will fetch my umbrella and walk up to the gate-house with you," said Miss Araminter briskly. "You go back to bed, my dears. I will return directly."

"Thank you, ma'am," said Mrs. Burdock. A tear trickled down her face.

Miss Araminter put her arm around Mrs. Burdock. "I'm sure they will find him safe," she said again, and patted her shoulder.

⁕

Stella lay awake in bed for a long time, listening to the pouring rain and the moaning wind. Thunder rumbled.

Her bed was lumpy and uncomfortable. She turned over with a sigh. Poor Jem. Out in the rain and the dark, lost or hurt.

Or something worse.

She remembered a depressing story from *A Garden of Lilies*. Instead of hurrying straight home from school, Roderick and Sapphira loitered with some other children, playing marbles, and were snatched up and carried away by a gigantic bird.

> *Boys and girls who stop and play,*
> *Won't live to see another day.*

Stella sighed. *A Garden of Lilies* was a truly miserable book.

She hoped Jem was safe. Perhaps the searching men had already found him. Perhaps right now he was at home, sleeping in his own bed in the gatehouse.

She thought about the monster. She didn't want to, but it was there in her mind, a dark shadow lurking in the wood. She imagined Jem being crunched up, bones and all, like the missing sheep. The thought was like a cold stone lodged in her insides.

"Where is he?" she whispered to Letty. But Letty did not answer.

Stella shivered. She heaved the covers over her head, curled up, and closed her eyes. Just as she was falling asleep, she remembered the white, frightened face that she had glimpsed in the flash of lightning, and the wispy, clutching fingers that had gripped her hand in the darkness.

·❦ Eighteen ❦·

When Stella woke, her head felt thick and heavy, as if she had been crying. It was daylight. Hortense's bed was empty. She sat up and touched her forehead. It did not hurt very much, unless she poked it quite hard. She untied the poultice, picked off the bits of leaf, and inspected her foot. The bruise had faded. It felt much better. She got out of bed, pulled back the curtains, and looked out of the window. The rain had stopped, but it was a cold, gray morning. Water dripped from the gutters, and the garden was sodden and battered from the storm.

She thought about Jem as she washed and dressed, pulling on warm stockings and two thick woolen petticoats. She hoped the men had found him during the night. Perhaps right now Jem was safely back home, being scolded by Mrs. Burdock. Twisting around, Stella quickly buttoned up the back of her dress and went down to the kitchen.

Miss Araminter, Strideforth, and Hortense were eating breakfast. Henry was sitting on Hortense's lap like a large, ill-tempered cushion. She had her arms around him and was stroking the soft feathers on his front.

Strideforth offered Stella an apple and a piece of bread and jam. "Jem's still missing," he said. "They searched all night, and they're still searching, but they haven't found him yet. Mrs. Burdock says the police are coming over from Brockley."

"Oh no," said Stella. She sat down at the table.

Strideforth nodded. "The police detectives will search for clues. It is very scientific. They will find him, that is certain."

Miss Araminter said, "How are you feeling this morning, my dear?"

"Much better, thank you."

Miss Araminter examined Stella's forehead and foot, said "Splendid," and wrote something in her notebook. "All the same, no lessons for you today. Rest quietly and read."

So after breakfast, while Strideforth had a Latin lesson and Hortense studied the properties of spleenworts, Stella curled up in the armchair beside the range to read Wilberforce Montgomery's journal. It was difficult to concentrate, partly because she kept thinking about Jem, and partly because Henry was stamping up and down on the table in a distracting manner, flapping his wings and shouting things in Latin. Stella turned the pages of the journal slowly and looked at the pictures. Wilberforce Montgomery was still exploring the caves in Madagascar, venturing deeper, encountering bats and glowworms and strange pale spiders. She turned another page and gasped.

It was a drawing of the creature from the lake. She recognized its wide, flat head and wicked-looking teeth. But it was not a fish. It had four short legs with webbed feet and a long, tapering tail.

The paper looked as if it had been soaked in muddy water. The ink had run and the writing was particularly difficult to read. Stella followed the words with her finger: . . . *live in fear of . . . Venomous Bite . . . the Natives believe has the power to . . . I witnessed the Transformation and I was Astounded . . . Petrified . . . After much exertion, I have obtained an Egg . . . hatch underground . . . darkness . . .*

The next page was torn out, and on the following was a recipe for a pudding made from cocoa-nut milk, turtles' eggs, and Oxford marmalade. Stella turned back to the drawing of the creature. "'Venomous Bite,'" she whispered.

Strideforth and Hortense looked up from their books.

"Oh, I am sorry to interrupt, Miss Araminter," said Stella. "But look. This is what we saw in the lake." She showed them the drawing.

Strideforth said, "That is not a fish at all. Fish do not have legs."

"Wilberforce Montgomery brought an egg back from Madagascar. It must have hatched."

"Is it a crocodile?" asked Strideforth.

Miss Araminter examined the drawing and said, "I should think it is one of the larger salamanders. From Madagascar, you say? I am not acquainted with any African species. How marvelous if it has been living here in the lake all this time."

"A salamander. Is that a lizard?" asked Stella.

"An amphibian, my dear. Similar to a frog."

Stella swallowed. "Are they dangerous?" she asked. "A-are they venomous?"

"Goodness, no. Quite harmless."

Stella remembered the dark shape sliding through the water lilies and the rows of needlelike teeth glinting in the mist. "It says 'Venomous Bite.' It couldn't— I mean, it couldn't turn something into stone? A fish?"

"Whatever are you thinking, my dear? No, no. Of course, some species do grow rather large. The hellbender. The olm. The mudpuppy. The giant salamander resides in China and can reach six feet in length. I imagine it could deliver a nasty nip, if provoked." Miss Araminter smiled and turned back to the Latin lesson.

Stella met Strideforth's gaze. The creature in the lake was much larger and much more dangerous than that.

⁓ ⚬ ⁓

They had cheese sandwiches and apples for dinner. Afterward, Miss Araminter inspected Stella's foot again and agreed that she might walk to the village with Strideforth and Hortense to collect the bread and milk. "But do not tire yourself, my dear. When you reach the village, you must promise to stop and rest."

They pulled on their coats and hats and went out. Henry's angry screams echoed from inside the house. Strideforth swung the empty milk can. Their feet crunched on the wet gravel as they went up the drive. Somewhere in the garden, a peacock gave a harsh cry.

Mrs. Burdock came out to unlock the gate for them. Her face was pale, and her eyes were red, as if she had been crying.

"Is there any news?" asked Stella.

Mrs. Burdock shook her head. "Keep to the road," she said. "Do you hear me? And mind you're back home before dark."

"Poor Jem," said Stella as they walked along the winding lane. "What can have happened to him?"

Gray clouds filled the sky, like ink spreading across wet paper. They passed a group of sheep huddled together in a corner of a muddy field. Hortense bleated at them and they answered her with nervous cries.

When they reached the village, Strideforth hesitated outside the post office. "I'll just go in and see if a letter has come," he said, and went inside. He came out a few minutes later, empty-handed, and shrugged. "Nothing, again. Will you wait here and rest, Stella? Hortense and I will get the bread and milk."

Stella sat down on the seat outside the post office. People were clustered in anxious groups, or scurrying along the street with their heads down.

"Dragging the Yarrow Canal, they are. But if the poor lad went in there—"

"Dreadful, altogether."

"The police sent for, and all."

"I said it would happen again. I said. After last time—"

"Hush!"

Stella turned to look. A woman caught her eye, whispered something to her companions, and they all looked at Stella, then turned and hurried away. She watched them go. *After last time.* What did that mean?

She looked across the green. Two large, shaggy horses were harnessed to the dentist's wagon. Mr. Flint was watching and directing as a young man carried boxes out from the tent and put them inside. Another youth was up a ladder, taking down the strings of flags. A third was loosening the ropes and pulling the tent pegs out of the ground. Mr. Flint glanced up, met Stella's gaze, lifted his hat to her, and gave a mocking bow. Stella looked away, but she could

feel his green, glinting eyes watching her. The back of her neck prickled. After a moment, she stood up and walked away along the street, pretending to be interested in the shop windows. She stopped outside the grocer's and gazed in an attentive manner at the boxes and tins of anchovies, knife polish, and soap.

She heard shuffling footsteps approaching and half turned away from the window. Someone blundered into her, spinning her around, nearly knocking her over. It was Mrs. Spindleweed.

"I'm sorry," Stella gasped, but the old woman did not answer as she hurried on past the ironmonger's and disappeared down the alley that led to the sweetshop. After a moment, the bell jangled. Stella ventured down the alley after her. The air smelled of peppermint and licorice. Shutters were over the windows. Tentatively Stella turned the door handle. It was locked. From above, she heard a faint cry. A kitten, perhaps. Or a small bird. She stepped back and looked at the upstairs windows. The curtains were drawn and the windows were dark, but she had the strange feeling that someone was watching her. An owl hooted. Stella shivered. Nervously she backed away, almost tripping over her feet, and hurried along the alley to the street.

Strideforth and Hortense were waiting for her

outside the post office. Strideforth carried the can of milk and Hortense held a large loaf of bread wrapped in paper.

"There you are," said Strideforth. "Where did you go? How is your foot? Have you had enough rest? We should go home, I think, before it starts raining."

"Yes, I'm fine. Here. Let me help." She took the bread from Hortense and tucked it under her arm. Hortense gave her a tiny smile.

"They are searching for Jem over at Yarrow," said Strideforth as they headed out of the village.

"I heard people say he might have fallen into the canal," said Stella. "I do hope he hasn't drowned. I wish we could help find him."

"Yes," agreed Strideforth. "We could help, I'm sure. We could search for clues, like the police detectives."

After a moment or two, Stella said, "Did you see that Mr. Flint is packing up his tent?"

"I suppose he has pulled out all the sore teeth in the village," said Strideforth.

The gray clouds were darkening overhead, and an icy wind blew across the fields. As they crossed the bridge, Stella looked down the hill to the dark shape of Boggart Wood in the valley below. She said, "Jem thought the monster was in the wood."

Strideforth stopped and looked down at the wood. "Perhaps he went to look for it."

"He might have."

"Let's go and see." Strideforth passed the milk can to Hortense and scrambled down the bank. "He said there was a track beside the stream." He disappeared into the undergrowth. There were scrabbling and crashing sounds. "Yes," he called. "Here it is."

Stella and Hortense clambered down the bank, pushing their way through the overgrown hedgerow. They found a cart track, almost hidden in straggling brambles and blackthorns.

Strideforth said, "Let's leave the milk and bread here. We can pick them up when we come back." He took the milk can and the loaf of bread and tucked them into the hedgerow. "Come on." He led the way, searching the ground as he went. "This is what the police detectives would do," he said over his shoulder. "Look for evidence—footprints and bloodstains. The smallest thing might be a clue."

The cart track wound down the hill, following the splashing, tumbling stream. They walked between the muddy wheel ruts, pushing through clumps of weeds. As they approached the wood, Stella shivered and hugged her coat more tightly around herself. It was a dense tangle of trees, crowded together. The wintry branches made spiky shapes against the gray sky. It was easy to believe that monsters and ghosts could be hiding in the shadows. Stella remembered that Jem always whistled a tune when he went near the wood. She hummed under her breath.

They poked around in the swampy thickets at the edge of the trees, looking for clues. There had been a fence once, but it had rotted and fallen down. They found several clusters of large mushrooms, a broken cartwheel, and an abandoned rusty bedstead.

Suddenly Anya squeaked. She leaped from Hortense's shoulder up onto an overhanging branch. Hortense tried to catch her, but she darted away like quicksilver. Chittering, she leaped onto another tree, scampered down the trunk, and disappeared into a tangle of brambles.

They followed her, shoving into the undergrowth beside the track.

Strideforth pushed the brambles aside. "Ouch," he said, sucking his finger. "She bit me."

Hortense caught Anya and held her tightly as she wriggled and squeaked.

"Look," said Strideforth, pointing. Jem's tallybag was snagged on a bramble, hanging from a broken bootlace. Strideforth untwisted it carefully from the prickles.

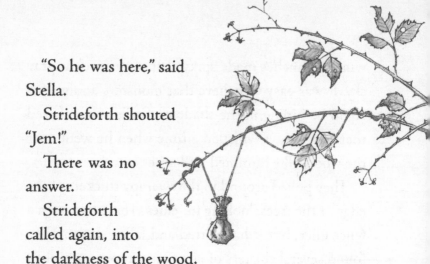

"So he was here," said Stella.

Strideforth shouted "Jem!"

There was no answer.

Strideforth called again, into the darkness of the wood. "Jem! Jem! Are you there? Jem!"

The only sounds were the trickling water and the wind stirring the dead leaves on the branches overhead.

❧ Nineteen ❧

They looked at one another uneasily.

"He must have gone into the wood," said Stella.

"We should go back and get help," said Strideforth.

"But he might be close by. He might be hurt," said Stella.

Strideforth pushed the tallybag into his pocket. "Well, we can just go a short way. If we follow the track, we can't get lost. Come on."

It was dark under the trees, and very cold and still. Moss and dead leaves muffled their footsteps. The branches of the trees were tangled with ivy and clumps of mistletoe. The twigs were like the spindly fingers of old men, reaching overhead, blocking out the daylight.

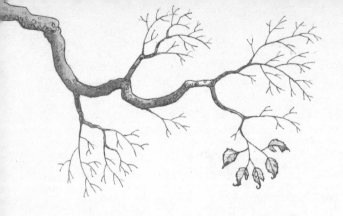

Stella remembered Jem saying, *If you go in, you might never come out again.*

They went along slowly, keeping close together. Strideforth stopped. "Look!" In a patch of mud in the middle of the track was the print of a nailed boot. "Smaller than mine," he said, comparing his foot. "It's Jem's."

Strideforth searched the ground for more clues. They clambered over a fallen tree trunk. Anya sniffed the air and made a sharp, chittering cry, her fur spiky. Strideforth stopped again. Half-hidden in the tangled undergrowth beside the track were three frightened sheep, huddled together.

Stella approached them, holding her breath. The sheep were motionless. She reached out and touched the back of one of them. It was cold and hard.

Strideforth felt it. "Stone," he whispered.

Hortense looked into the sheep's face and stroked its head. The sheep stared back at her with sightless stone eyes.

Strideforth frowned at the sheep. After a moment he said, "It's just like that goldfish, isn't it? It's just the same."

Stella nodded. She swallowed.

"It's the creature from the lake. It poisons things and turns them into stone," said Strideforth. "It is the monster. That is certain."

"But how did it get here from the lake?" asked Stella. She remembered the picture in the journal. The wide black head and the rows of wicked teeth. "And where's Jem?"

"Do you think he went after it? Perhaps he followed it farther into the wood. But what if he—" Strideforth did not finish.

Something moved in the undergrowth nearby. They looked at one another.

"Jem!" they called. "Jem! Jem!" Their voices seemed to be swallowed up by the silence and the shadows.

They called again. There was no answer.

Strideforth hesitated, then said, "I think we should go and get help."

"Yes," agreed Stella.

Hortense nodded.

They started back the way they had come. The wood seemed darker, as if the trees were leaning toward them. A startled bird took flight with a clatter of wings, and Stella jumped, her heart thumping. Something rustled. She turned around, but there was nothing to see.

In *A Garden of Lilies*, Tilly and Ursula strayed into a herbaceous border during a Sunday school picnic. All that was ever found of them was a hair ribbon.

> *Wandering children should beware*
> *Of dangers lurking everywhere.*

Stella swallowed and walked a little faster, humming to herself under her breath.

She heard another sound and spun around.

Something moved, sliding through the ferns.

Strideforth grasped Hortense by the hand. "Run!"

They fled, leaping and scrambling over fallen branches and tree roots. Stella's feet skidded in the moss and mud. Brambles scratched at her stockings. Twigs snagged in her hair.

Gasping, they sprinted headlong out of the wood. Stella looked behind, panting. Nothing followed them.

"Come on," said Strideforth.

They clambered up the hill toward the lane. As they stopped to collect the bread and milk, Stella looked back. Down in the valley, the wood was a dark, crouching shape.

⚬⚬⚬

When they reached the gates of Wormwood Mire, Mrs. Burdock was waiting for them. She unlocked the gate and pulled it open.

"Mrs. Burdock, look," Strideforth said. He showed her Jem's tallybag. "We found this. It's Jem's. We found it in Boggart Wood. And his footprint, too." He took a breath. "We went in and found the sheep. And they were—"

Mrs. Burdock saw the tallybag and staggered backward, her face white. "In Boggart Wood? I told him to keep away. I told him and told him." Her voice was shaking.

Mr. Burdock came around the side of the gate-house. He grunted. "Gone in the wood, is he?" He nodded and went inside. He came out a moment later, wearing his coat and carrying a lantern and a long stick.

"Where?" he asked.

Strideforth explained that they had followed the cart track down the hill. "We found the tallybag at the edge of the wood and went in a little way. And we saw—"

"I'll let them know in the village," said Mr. Burdock. His face was set and grim. He laid a hand on Mrs. Burdock's arm. "Don't fret. We'll find him."

"I'll help search," said Strideforth eagerly. "I can show you where we found the clues and where the—"

"No," said Mr. Burdock grimly. "No children. Stay inside." He turned and strode away along the lane toward the village.

Strideforth watched him go. "I'm sure I could help," he said, downcast.

Mrs. Burdock was shaking. Stella put her arm around her, Strideforth supported her other side, and with some difficulty, they steered her to the gatehouse, through the narrow front door into a small, dark parlor, and sat her down in a chair beside the fire.

"We need Miss Araminter," Stella said. She looked at Mrs. Burdock's white face.

Strideforth nodded. "We'll go and get her

straightaway," he said. "Will you wait here? Will you be all right?"

"Yes," said Stella. "Be quick."

Strideforth and Hortense hurried away. Stella heard their footsteps on the gravel drive outside.

She said tentatively, "I'm sure Jem will be home soon."

Mrs. Burdock did not seem to hear. Stella twisted her fingers together. What if the creature had bitten Jem and turned him into a statue, like the stone sheep? Cold and hard, with sightless stone eyes?

Tea, she thought. Whenever the Aunts were upset by something, which was rather often, they rang for tea. She pushed open a door on the other side of the parlor, went along a passageway, and came to a small kitchen. Stella had never made the tea herself, but she had watched Ada do it hundreds of times. She filled the kettle from the pump and put it on the range. She poked around in the cupboards and found the tea in a tin with a picture of the queen on it. She put three heaped spoonfuls of tea into the pot, hesitated, and then added two more spoonfuls. When the kettle boiled, she filled the teapot. She found a cup and saucer. She poured tea into the cup and looked at it doubtfully. It was rather darker than the tea Ada usually made. She added some milk and

a big spoonful of sugar. She stirred the tea carefully and carried it back to the parlor.

Mrs. Burdock took the cup and pointed a shaking finger toward the mantelpiece. "My tonic," she said.

Stella searched along the cluttered mantelpiece. There was a candlestick, a tin of tobacco, a clock, a china parrot, two china dogs, a jar of boot polish, a photograph of a sailor, and a bundle of letters and vegetable seed packets. Behind the papers was a black bottle with a cork in it. "This?" she asked.

Mrs. Burdock nodded, took the bottle, pulled the cork out with her teeth, and splashed a good measure into the tea. She took a mouthful, and the color began to return to her face.

Stella pushed the bundle of papers into place on  the mantelpiece. Something lay at the back of the shelf. It was a battered little wooden doll. It had jointed arms and legs, a painted face, and a faded yellow dress. Its hair was worn away.

Stella picked it up. It fitted into her hand as if it belonged there.

Letty's doll.

She gasped. "Mrs. Burdock, what—"

Mrs. Burdock drew in a ragged breath. She said, "Take it."

"But—"

"I kept it to remind me." Her voice faltered. "But I won't ever forget, will I? You take it." Her eyes filled with tears. "We should never have stayed, after it happened. We should have moved far away. I told Jem to keep away from the wood, I did. I told him and told him. I thought I could keep him safe. But I'm so afraid we'll never see him again."

Stella sat down, clutching the little doll. "I'm sure they will find him."

Mrs. Burdock shook her head. She took another gulp of tea. After a moment, she said, "It's happening again. Just the same. Gone. Just like that poor young lady and the two little girls."

Stella whispered, "My mother. What happened to her?"

"Sad, she was. Waiting for someone, I thought, but if she was, he never came. And if he had, we weren't to let him in, anyway. The gate locked, always. No visitors. Those were the orders." She looked at Stella and sighed.

"What happened to her?" asked Stella again.

"We searched the house and the garden. They dragged the lake and all. We din't find her. Not a trace. Then the strangest thing. One of the little ones turned up. Wandering all alone, crying, right in the middle of Boggart Wood." She looked at Stella. "You, that was. Nobody knew how you got there. Uncanny. That's what folks said. No sign of the young lady, or the other little one. Dead and gone, they were." She nodded at the little doll in Stella's hand. "They found that in the wood. That's all they ever found. And everyone talking about this monster. It's just the same, all over again." A tear rolled down her face. "And now my poor boy's gone the same way. Dead and gone in Boggart Wood."

"I'm sure they will find him," said Stella again. She reached out and touched Mrs. Burdock's hand. She had so many questions to ask. "What was my mother like? Why was she here?"

Mrs. Burdock shook her head once more. "I promised I'd keep it secret."

"But what—?" Stella was interrupted by a knock at the door, and Miss Araminter strode in, followed by Strideforth and Hortense.

The governess was carrying an armful of plants. She said, "Pennyroyal, poppy, and wormwood. And a few leaves from the Mongolian carpet berry."

Mrs. Burdock looked up. Her face was wet with tears.

Miss Araminter swooped down and patted her shoulder. "There, there, Mrs. Burdock. I will make you a tisane. It will help you sleep." She turned and said, "Hurry home now, my dears, and have your tea. I will sit here with Mrs. Burdock and wait for news."

ಆ Twenty ಶಾ

*I*n the late afternoon, the towers and chimneys of Wormwood Mire made a looming, jagged shape against the gray sky. As they walked down the drive toward the house, Stella told Strideforth and Hortense what Mrs. Burdock had said about her mother and her sister. How they had disappeared all those years ago, and how Stella had been found, all alone, in Boggart Wood. She showed them Letty's little doll.

"What do you think happened to them?" asked Strideforth. "And why were you in the wood? How did you get there?"

"I don't know," said Stella. "Mrs. Burdock said something about a secret, but I don't know what she meant." She imagined herself as a small child, wandering amongst the dark trees, crying. She could not remember it at all.

Up in her bedroom, she held the two little dolls side by side. Her doll and Letty's doll. They were battered and worm-eaten. Her doll had only a few strands of hair on its head, and Letty's doll had no hair at all. Their dresses were moldy and faded and torn. But they had once been identical. Like twins.

Stella opened the musical box, took out the photograph, and looked at the two babies in the perambulator. She remembered playing on the floor of the nursery with Letty, listening to the whispering, tinkling tune. Tiny specks of dust had danced and shimmered in the air.

She thought about what Mrs. Burdock had said: *Dead and gone.*

A tear trickled down her cheek. It had been very comforting to have a sister, even an imaginary one. Letty had made Stella feel braver. Everything was easier when there were two of you.

But Letty had been dead for ten years, and Stella did not even know her real name. She might never discover what happened to her.

Stella wiped her eyes. It was foolish to cry about something that had happened so long ago. She put the photograph back into the musical box and laid the two little dolls on top of it. She stroked them with the tip of her finger and looked at them for a moment. Then she closed the lid with a snap and pushed the box into the pocket of her dress.

She took a deep breath and stared at her reflection in the mirror.

Right now, she should not be thinking about Letty. She should be thinking about Jem. He was real, and he was in terrible danger. Lost in Boggart Wood where the monster, the salamander, was lurking, biting things and turning them into stone. What if Jem was already a statue, just like the goldfish and the sheep? It was a dreadful thought.

She had to help him, if she could. Perhaps she could learn something more about the monster. Where it was hiding. How to catch it. Maybe there was something useful in Wilberforce Montgomery's journal. She snatched it up and hurried down to the kitchen.

Strideforth and Hortense were making cocoa and sandwiches. Henry and Anya were squabbling over a tin of sardines.

"I should be helping to find Jem," Strideforth said as he spread jam on the ragged slices of bread. "I could have shown them where we found the tallybag and the footprint and the sheep. I could have found more clues. That is certain."

"I hope he is safe," said Stella. "I hope they find him soon." She helped make the cocoa, and then carried her cup and a sandwich to the table, sat down, and opened the journal. She found the drawing of the salamander again and ran her finger from its wide black head to its tapering tail. She tilted the page toward the light, trying to make out more of the words, but the writing was too faint. *I witnessed the Transformation and I was Astounded . . .*

Stella took a bite of her sandwich and turned the pages of the journal, looking at the pictures and skimming through the words, searching for any information that might be useful.

It was warm in the kitchen. Hortense sat cross-legged on the floor, feeding crumbs to Teasel and a family of mice as Anya watched jealously from the top of her head. On the mantelpiece, Henry was shrieking happily and tearing Strideforth's Latin preparation to shreds. Strideforth frowned and kicked the leg of the table.

Stella turned another page. Wilberforce Montgomery was in the South Seas, attempting to wrestle an enormous tropical octopus into a huge tank. *I am determined to add it to my Secret Collection, but the Creature is reluctant to be Confined. I suffered a number of painful Stings.* She read on, turning page after page. She followed Wilberforce Montgomery as he sailed through the tropical seas in an outrigger canoe. He climbed mountains, and crossed glaciers and deserts and jungles and oceans, but he wrote nothing more about the monster. She reached the end of the journal at last and closed it with a snap. "Nothing," she said. "I'm going to look in his study. There might be a book about salamanders."

"There might be," agreed Strideforth. "You should take the lantern. It will be getting dark soon." He rocked his chair back and stared up at the heating pipes. "Did you hear that?"

"What?" asked Stella.

"Banging. Can't you hear it?" said Strideforth. "Where is it coming from?" He shoved the chair across the room, climbed onto it, and put his ear to one of the pipes. He tapped it with his finger. "I'm going to look at the furnace."

Stella picked up the lantern and set off for the library. On the way, she stopped to look at the painting of Wilberforce Montgomery again. He still sat in the little Egyptian summerhouse beside the lake, smiling. His black eyes seemed to twinkle with mischief. Stella frowned at him. He had no reason to look so cheerful. He had caused so much trouble, collecting dangerous creatures and bringing them here.

She went on, her footsteps echoing in the dusty passages and empty rooms, to the library. She

climbed the iron staircase, slipped through the secret
door behind the bookcase, and went along the passageway and up the stairs to the tower.

Stella looked around. She could imagine Wilberforce Montgomery sitting at his desk here, all those
years ago, reading his journal, dreaming about his
adventures. The study was warm. The heating pipes
clanked and hissed. The giant crab and the stuffed
crocodile and the dead seedpods and tendrils of the
strangler vine dangled overhead, making strange
shadows on the ceiling. Outside, an owl hooted as
it flew past the tower. Stella could see a faint light
glimmering in the window of the gatehouse at the
top of the drive, where Mrs. Burdock and Miss Araminter were sitting in the little parlor, waiting for
news about Jem.

She put the lantern down on the desk and ran her
finger along a row of books, searching for one that
might contain information about salamanders. *Wan-
derings in Wisconsin. To Damascus by Dirigible.* At
the end of the lowest shelf was a small green volume,
A Treasury of Amphibians. It was full of little colored

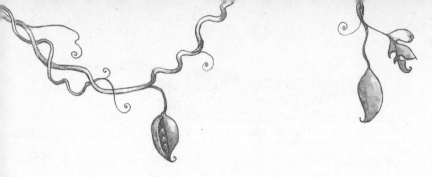

pictures and anecdotes about all kinds of frogs and toads. She leafed through the pages and found a picture of a small, lizardlike creature.

The Salamander or Newt is a distant cousin of the frog and inhabits ponds, ditches, and caves. It hibernates in the cold and ventures out only when the weather is warm and agreeable. It is nocturnal, has poor eyesight, and no external ears. It hunts prey, such as tadpoles, slugs, and earthworms, by sensing the vibrations caused by movement.

Stella read the passage through twice and looked at the picture closely. The little creature did not look much like the monster; it was only a few inches long and was decorated with cheerful spots. She searched through the book, but there was nothing more about salamanders. She was pushing it back into place when she heard voices and footsteps.

"Stella!" Strideforth and Hortense climbed up into the study. Henry was riding on Hortense's head. "Stella, come quickly! Come and see what I found," said Strideforth.

She picked up the lantern and followed them

down the passageway and through the library. She caught up with them in the entrance hall. Strideforth turned around and walked backward, almost tripping over his feet in his hurry. "I heard something banging in the pipes," he said. "And I found out where it's coming from." He rushed on, leading the way through the house to the servants' wing and then down into the cellar, where the huge furnace was clanking and moaning and emitting bursts of steam.

"Look." Strideforth was out of breath. "See these pipes here?" He waved at the iron pipes that snaked out of the furnace and disappeared into the ceiling. "They go up into the main bedrooms, the ballroom, and everywhere." He looked at Stella to see that she was paying attention. She nodded. "They go everywhere around the house. I've followed them. I know where they all go."

Stella nodded again.

"Now, come and look at this." Strideforth squeezed behind the furnace. Stella and Hortense followed him, ducking underneath a row of shiny brass dials and levers. Strideforth edged his way along the wall, crouched down, and pointed to a large pipe that emerged from the back of the furnace and disappeared into the wall behind. He touched it gingerly.

"It's very hot. There is a lot of heat going somewhere." He wrapped a piece of rag around the pipe and put his ear against it. He beckoned Stella closer. "Listen," he said.

She knelt down. Even through the rag, the pipe was hot against her ear. She could hear a dull, muffled roar. A hiss. Distant clanging and thumping sounds. Then she heard something echoing along the pipe. It was cheerful and piercing, but very faint. Someone was whistling.

"Jem!" she gasped.

Strideforth nodded vigorously. "Yes. I don't think he can hear us, though. I shouted as loudly as I could, and he did not answer. But listen to this." He picked up a piece of rusty metal and banged it against the pipe. *Clang, clang.*

After a few seconds, from somewhere far away, came an answer. *Clang, clang.*

Strideforth hit the pipe again. *Clang.*

Clang came the reply immediately. Then a whole series of frantic clangs and bangs echoed in the pipe.

Henry shrieked and flapped his wings, making them all duck. Anya squeaked and chittered and

danced up and down, twisting her body like a snake.

Strideforth said, "So then I followed the pipe." He pushed open a low door, ducked through it, and led them into another cellar, full of old barrels, broken furniture, and cobwebs. "I thought it might lead outside to the stables. Wilberforce Montgomery might have heated them because of the zebras and other animals he had here. But it does not. Look." He pointed.

In a dark corner of the cellar, the pipe made a turn and disappeared straight down into the floor.

"It goes underground. Jem is trapped down there somewhere. We have to find the way down."

❧ Twenty-One ❧

They searched all the cellars, looking for forgotten doors or staircases. They heaved the broken furniture aside and examined the floor for trapdoors. Stella rapped on the flagstones, listening for hollow sounds. Strideforth jammed his pocketknife into gaps in the walls to find loose bricks. Hortense ventured into dark corners, looking for cavities.

"Nothing," said Strideforth.

They climbed the stairs and searched the larder and the shoe room and the knife room and the still-room and the butler's pantry and the water closet and the scullery and the kitchen.

Strideforth rubbed a grimy hand through his hair. He was covered with dust and cobwebs and looked discouraged. He sat down with a thump on a chair at the kitchen table, taking a bite of a leftover jam sandwich. "We need to think," he said with his mouth full. "That pipe leads underground. If there is a room below the cellar, there must be a way down to it."

Stella and Hortense sat down opposite him. Stella said, "Perhaps there is a secret door, like the one in the library."

Strideforth asked, "But where is it?"

Stella considered for a moment. "Well, if Wilberforce Montgomery built a secret door leading to a secret underground room, he wouldn't have made it here in the servants' wing. Jem said he had lots of servants. They would have noticed if he came down here."

"That's true." Strideforth nodded. "Mrs. Burdock said he was always in the library. Perhaps it is there?"

Stella thought about the portrait of Wilberforce Montgomery sitting in his summerhouse, his beady black eyes twinkling with laughter. Suddenly she remembered that night, all those years ago, hurrying through the garden in the dark, clutching her mother's hand. She had dropped her doll. Her mother had pulled her past. And then they had gone down. Down into darkness.

She said, "No, not the library. The summerhouse."

"What? Why?"

She stood up. "That's what I remember. When I was little, we went into the summerhouse, and then, somehow, we went down. It must be there. Come on."

Strideforth pushed the remains of his sandwich into his pocket and jumped to his feet.

They pulled on their coats. Henry shrieked and flapped across the kitchen, landing on Hortense's head with a thump. Strideforth picked up the lantern and they went out into the dusk. They hurried across the yard, around the stables, through the orchard, and down the slippery, wet steps toward the lake. The garden was full of spiky shapes and shadows. Tendrils of mist drifted across the surface of the water. A frog croaked. A peacock gave a mournful cry. In the undergrowth, a lightning beetle sparked and flashed. They followed the path around the lake toward the summerhouse, past the waterfall, and across the bridge.

Strideforth stopped. "What's that?"

"What?"

He watched the lake for a moment and then shrugged. "I thought something moved. Just a fish, perhaps."

They went on, ducking under dripping leaves, splashing through puddles. They reached the summerhouse. Stella stood in the middle of the damp, shadowy little room and looked around, trying to remember exactly what had happened all those years ago.

"It was dark," she said. "We were hurrying, and we had to be very quiet. I dropped my doll. I couldn't find it, but my mother would not stop. Someone was crying, I think. And then we went down. Right here. Down and down, into the dark." She looked at the floor of the summerhouse. "Right here," she repeated doubtfully. The floor was covered with mud and dead leaves and moss, and little curling ferns and clusters of toadstools. It looked extremely solid.

Strideforth kicked a few of the leaves aside. Underneath were tiny colored tiles. They knelt down and cleared away the debris with their hands, uncovering an intricate mosaic, a pattern of beetles and birds and strange Egyptian symbols made from hundreds of colored tiles and shells and pebbles and sparkling pieces of mirror. In the middle was a two-headed snake, coiled in a circle. Its scales glinted like the wings of beetles.

Stella frowned at the mosaic pattern. It reminded her of something.

Strideforth squinted sideways along the floor. He rapped it with his knuckles. He fished out his pocketknife, opened a blade, and poked it between the tiles. "I don't know," he said. "There is no hidden door. There is nothing here."

Stella remembered something from Wilberforce Montgomery's journal. He had been exploring inside a pyramid in Egypt and found the way into a secret tomb. (*The doorway was hidden in a marvelously ingenious manner.*) He had made a careful drawing of the mechanism that unlocked the door. It had opened when he had pressed the eyes of a carving of a two-headed serpent.

She touched the mosaic snake's eyes. They were made from glossy black stones, as round and smooth as marbles. She held her breath and pressed them both, as hard as she could. There was a click.

Something creaked under the floor. Henry shrieked and flapped his wings. They all jumped to their feet and backed away. A section of the floor lifted up, and then, with an earsplitting scraping, grinding sound, it slowly swiveled aside, revealing a hole and a flight of rusty iron stairs, spiraling down into darkness.

They gaped in astonishment.

"How did you know to do that?" asked Strideforth.

"I read about it in Wilberforce Montgomery's journal," Stella said. "There was a tomb in Egypt. He must have copied it."

Strideforth knelt and peered down into the hole. "It's very interesting. Look. There is a hidden catch. When you pressed the eyes, it moved these levers here, and the counterweight fell, and that made it slide across." He poked at the rusty mechanism.

Stella crouched beside him. The air in the hole was warm and smelled of drains and mildew. "Jem?" she called. "Jem? Are you down there?"

Her voice echoed back up to them.

They looked at one another nervously.

Stella remembered a story from *A Garden of Lilies*. Victoria, Wilfreda, and Xavier went into a tunnel of some kind, and then they were eaten by a crocodile or fell into an abyss or something else dreadful happened to them. Stella refused to think about it. This was not the time for horrible, discouraging stories.

She picked up the lantern and stepped onto the iron staircase. It creaked under her weight. She took a determined breath. "Come on," she said, and climbed down into the hole.

Strideforth and Hortense followed her. The stairs spiraled down and down. At the bottom was an arched brick tunnel. They ventured along it, keeping close together. Their footsteps echoed. Water dripped. The lantern light glistened on the puddles that stretched across the muddy floor.

"Look," whispered Strideforth. "We're under the lake."

Small round windows were set in the curved ceiling of the tunnel. Dim light filtered down through the murky water, making faint rippling reflections. Stella watched the shadowy shapes of the water lilies overhead. A school of little fish darted past. It was a strange, oppressive feeling, to be walking underneath the water. Even Henry and Anya were quiet. Anya was curled around the back of Hortense's neck, peering out through her hair, and Henry stood on top of her head, his feathers ruffled, looking alert.

At the end of the tunnel, another spiral staircase led upward. As they climbed, the air became warmer. Anya chittered at a small creature that scuttled up the wall and disappeared into a crack between the bricks. There were noises ahead, clanks and hisses and the sound of running water.

The stairs ended. They followed another tunnel and came out into a huge dark cavern full of looming shapes and obstacles.

"What is this?" whispered Strideforth, peering into the darkness.

Iron stairs and ladders and walkways led between giant tanks of water, bigger than bathtubs. Pipes snaked everywhere. Wisps of steam drifted through the air. Water trickled and dripped and overflowed, forming puddles and gurgling away down drains in the floor.

A large tank nearby was clogged with waterweed, the rubbery stems tangled together like worms. An enormous vine crawled up the rough rock wall, its pale tendrils and leaves reaching up to the dim light that filtered down from tiny gratings in the ceiling, high above.

"This must be where Wilberforce Montgomery kept his secret collection, don't you think?" Stella said. "From all those years ago."

Strideforth nodded. "Foreign fish."

"And other things," said Stella. A small creature skittered along the ground, darted between their feet, and vanished into the shadows.

Hortense leaned over a tank and looked down into the water. A bubble rose to the surface and floated there, glinting.

"Jem?" called Strideforth. "Jem? Are you there?" His voice echoed around the cavern.

Something touched Stella's foot. She looked down. The pale creeper was curling around her ankle. She

yelped and backed away. "Watch out. It's a strangler vine."

The vine was crawling along the pipes, reaching blindly toward them. A waving tendril found Strideforth's wrist and wrapped around it. He jerked his arm free.

"Miss Araminter would like this," he said, grinning.

Suddenly Henry shrieked. Hortense was struggling. The strangler vine was around her neck. She clawed at her throat, gasping for breath.

"Hortense!" yelled Strideforth.

Anya gave a shrill squeak and attacked the plant. Stella tried to pull it away, but it was too tough to break, and it was tightening around Hortense's neck in a determined manner. A stalk wrapped around her arm and another snaked across her chest.

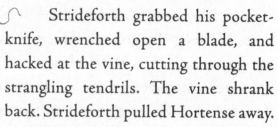

Strideforth grabbed his pocketknife, wrenched open a blade, and hacked at the vine, cutting through the strangling tendrils. The vine shrank back. Strideforth pulled Hortense away.

"Are you all right?" he asked.

Hortense nodded, rubbing her neck.

"Are you sure? Does it hurt?" Strideforth inspected Hortense's throat in the lantern light.

In the tank behind him, a sinuous shape slithered against the glass.

"Watch out!" said Stella.

He recoiled with a gasp. "What is that?"

"I don't know." Stella took a nervous breath, backing away from the tank and the strangler vine's waving tendrils. "Come on," she said. "If Jem is down here, we need to find him quickly and get out of here."

They made their way across the cavern, clambering over pipes, edging around tanks, and skirting puddles and drains. They passed a row of empty cages, their doors hanging open. Hortense stopped to peer inside, but Strideforth pulled her along.

In the middle of the cavern, they came to a huge pool of dark, rippling water. A narrow iron walkway led across to the other side. Stella eyed it doubtfully. It was rusty and looked rather unstable.

Strideforth crouched down and put his finger into the water. "Warm," he said. "This is where the water flows out into the lake, I think." He pointed to where the water swirled away down a wide drain. "That's why the lake is so warm—" He paused and said, "Listen."

There was a faint voice in the darkness.

"Jem!" Strideforth called. "Jem! Are you there?"

The voice answered. "Help! Help me!"

~ Twenty-Two ~

The rusty walkway creaked and shifted under their weight as they crossed the pool. The lantern light made wiggly reflections on the dark water. Stella could not tell how deep the pool was, and she certainly did not want to find out. She concentrated on keeping her balance until they reached the end of the walkway.

"Jem?" Strideforth called. "Jem?" His voice echoed around the cavern.

"Help!"

They threaded their way through pipes and machinery, peering up into the darkness.

"Where are you?" called Strideforth.

"Here!" The voice came from somewhere above.

Stella held the lantern as high as she could. "There he is," she gasped.

A large iron pipe ran down the wall of the cavern. Beside it was a rusty ladder. Most of it had fallen away from the wall and lay in bits on the ground.

A few rungs remained, fifteen feet overhead, dangling from broken bolts. Jem was clinging to them. His face was white and streaked with tears.

"Jem!" called Strideforth.

"Are you all right?" asked Stella.

"I'm stuck," he said, his voice shaking.

"How did you get up there?" asked Strideforth, gazing up at him.

"I climbed up. The ladder broke. I can't hang on. I'm going to fall." There was a creaking sound. Jem clung tighter. "Help!" he gasped.

"Don't let go. We'll get you down," called Strideforth. He looked around. "Perhaps we can drag this over." He grabbed part of the ladder that had fallen and tried to shove it across the floor. Stella put down the lantern and went to help him, but before they could move it closer, Hortense had pulled off her boots and stockings and was clambering up the wall. She was already overhead and climbing quickly, her toes and fingers finding tiny ledges and crevices in the rock. Henry flapped beside her,

"What if she falls?" whispered Stella.

"She won't fall," said Strideforth, without taking

his eyes off Hortense. "She is very, very good at climbing."

Hortense reached Jem and tried to make him let go of the broken ladder. He shook his head. She insisted, clucking at him, pulling him, until he released his grasp, first with one hand, and then the other. He clung like a limpet to the wall beside her.

Suddenly, with a scraping creak, the last bit of the ladder broke away from the wall and fell, end over end. Stella and Strideforth jumped out of the way. It hit the ground with an echoing clang.

Jem was shaking so much he nearly lost his grip on the wall. Hortense patted him, and then helped him climb down, supporting him, guiding his hands and feet, and making comforting, encouraging sounds all the way down.

They reached the ground, and Jem staggered and sat down on the floor. Stella let out the breath she had been holding. Strideforth grinned. He patted Jem on the back and hugged Hortense.

"Thank you," Jem said to Hortense.

She gave him a tiny smile.

"Are you all right?" Stella asked him.

"Have you got anything to eat? I'm clemmed."

Strideforth felt in his pockets and found half a jam sandwich. Jem took it and finished it in two famished bites.

"What happened? What are you doing down here?" asked Stella. "Did you find the secret trapdoor in the summerhouse too?"

"What trapdoor? I was in Boggart Wood. I reckoned I'd find the monster and follow it for a bit, and then I'd show Mr. Flint where it went and get that sovereign off him. I went a little way into the wood, along the old cart track, and I saw them missing sheep, and I reckon you won't believe this, but—"

"They'd been turned into stone," said Strideforth.

"Did you see them too? Gave me the frights, that did. What happened to them, do you reckon? It was right creepy in the wood, with them stone sheep. I remembered what people say: If you go into the wood, you might not come out again. And I thought about that ghost. The singing girl. I din't want to hear it singing. And then I saw my tallybag was gone." He touched his chest. "So I was going to run straight home, right then, quick as I could."

"I found it." Strideforth fished in his pocket and pulled it out. "I was looking for clues. Like the police detectives." Hortense frowned at him, and he said, "Well, Anya found it, really."

"She's right clever, ain't she?" Jem nodded at the little ermine on Hortense's shoulder as he knotted the broken bootlace and hung the bag around his neck. He tucked it under his shirt and patted it. "That's better," he said. "So, I was just about to run home, but then, all of a sudden, there's the monster. Cobbin' great thing. Black as a shadow. I ran like the clappers. It come after me, sliding along. I ran into the wood. The stream goes down a hole. Like a waterfall. And I fell down it." He laughed. "I tried to scramble up, but the rocks were slippery, and I fell right down to the bottom. It was deep and dark, and the monster was after me. So I went along underground for ages and ages, quick as I could, along these tunnels and caves, beside the stream. I had to wade in the water and squeeze between the rocks. It was horrible. I was whistling and whistling to keep safe. I kept going on and on, and then I come out there." He jerked a thumb over his shoulder toward a dark opening in the rock wall. A rusty pipe emerged from the opening, and water trickled from it into the pool. "Right warm it is here. I slept a bit. And then I whistled a bit. And then I heard noises in the pipe, next to my ear. So I kicked it, and then someone banged back."

"That was us," said Strideforth, grinning.

"I reckoned it was from somewhere up there. And I spied that ladder, and I climbed up. But then it broke. I clung on. I thought I was done for." He took a shuddering breath. "It's prime to see you."

"Everyone's worried about you," said Stella.

"They sent for the police," said Strideforth.

"Coo. Really?" Jem looked impressed.

"And Mrs. Burdock was crying," said Stella.

"Not Granny." Jem was unconvinced. "If I got bit by the monster, she'd say it served me right, I reckon. When she sees me, she'll wallop me into next week." He grinned cheerfully and looked around. "Where are we, anyway? What's all these pipes for?"

Strideforth picked up the lantern and peered into the darkness overhead. "I think we are right under the house. That is the heating pipe coming down from the furnace. It's heating up all these tanks and the water in that big pool and even the lake. No wonder it is burning so much coal." He poked at a row of rusty taps. "The stream comes out from the cave there and feeds into the pool. It's very interesting."

"In a book in the study, it said that salamanders hibernate in the cold," said Stella. "The monster was sleeping down here and the furnace must have woken it up. Whenever someone stays in the house, they turn on the furnace and the water down here warms up. Then the monster wakes up and it goes about biting things and scaring people."

Jem said, "Like a cobbin' tree trunk, it is. And all them teeth." He shuddered. "We don't want to meet it down here. Let's go."

Stella shivered. She pushed her hands into her pockets. "Ouch!" She felt a sharp scratch. She inspected the back of her wrist in the light of the lantern. Then she fished gingerly in her pocket and pulled out a small, curved thorn.

 Jem gasped. "That's a bloodthorn, that is."

"What's that?"

"Mrs. Spindleweed makes them," he said. "If a bloodthorn scratches you, you're bound to hurt yourself before next sunrise. People say she soaks them in her own blood to make them work."

"There's no such thing," said Strideforth. He took the little thorn with his finger and thumb and inspected it. "That's not scientific at all."

Jem shrugged. "Once, Seb Gromwell shouted something rude at Mrs. Spindleweed. So she scratched him on his hand here." He pointed. "It was only a tiny scratch. She did it passing him in the street, like that. And that same day, he got in a fight with George Oakapple, and Seb thumped him, and his whole hand swelled up. Just like a toad. I seen it."

Stella said, "But it can't be, really. Because I was scratched by a thorn like this before. Two times before. One was in my boot, and it scratched my foot just here, and one was in my hairbrush, and it scratched me here on my forehead." She touched her head and felt the fading bruise from hitting her head on the door. Her foot still ached a little. A shiver ran down her back, like a trickle of icy water. "Oh. But—"

Jem said, "Mrs. Spindleweed must've got it in for you."

Stella rubbed her wrist. "Why would she want to hurt me?" She remembered Mrs. Spindleweed's strange yellow eyes and her fingers, like the talons of a bird. "And how did she put the thorns in my boot and my pocket and my hairbrush? It's impossible."

"Maybe she got her owl to do it." Jem lowered his voice. "Or maybe her familiar."

Strideforth made an impatient noise in his throat. He flicked away the little thorn. "This is all non-sense. There's no such thing as familiars. They are just stories made up to frighten little children. That is certain. You should not believe things like that, Jem. Come on," he said. "We'll take you home now." He led the way back to the pool. They followed him along the creaking walkway, out over the water.

"I could eat a hot sausage, I could," said Jem conversationally. He smacked his lips. "A dozen sausages. And an oyster pie. And a cobbin' great bowl of Granny's rabbit stew. Or liver an' onions, with plenty of gravy. Or—"

Nearly halfway across, Strideforth stopped. "Listen," he said. There was a gurgling sound, like water running out of a bathtub. He lifted up the lantern and peered out across the rippling black water.

"What is it?" asked Stella.

Strideforth whispered, "I think something's coming up the drain."

A stream of bubbles appeared on the surface of the water. The ripples swirled. There were more gurgles. Then a dark shape slithered up from the drain and slid into the pool.

"The monster," gasped Jem. He clutched Stella's arm.

The walkway creaked and shifted.

Stella remembered the book in the study. "It hunts by sensing movement," she whispered. "So if we stay quite still, it won't know we're here."

They all froze.

The monster's wide head broke the surface of the water. Its skin gleamed in the lantern light. Its tiny eyes glittered.

Stella could feel Jem trembling. She felt for his hand and clasped it.

The monster swam across the pool, moving smoothly, slipping through the water, tail swishing slowly back and forth. Its back arched and it dived under the walkway, right beneath their feet.

Jem turned his head to watch it come up. He shifted his weight, and the walkway creaked.

The monster lunged like a striking snake, churning the water with a flick of its tail. Its mouth opened. Its teeth glinted.

Jem cried out and turned to run. He knocked the lantern from Strideforth's hand. It smashed, plunging them into darkness. Jem yelled and fell into the water. He struggled to the surface, spluttering and splashing. Stella and Strideforth and Hortense flung themselves down onto the walkway, groping for him. Stella grabbed one of his clutching, wet hands and a fistful of his hair. They hauled him out, coughing and gasping, and yanked him to his feet.

The walkway lurched. They all yelled. The monster had clambered up out of the water. It was a huge black shape in the darkness. It slithered toward them.

"We can't get past. We have to go back!" shouted Strideforth, "Quick. Run!"

They turned around and sprinted back along the walkway. It jerked and clattered.

"Come on," said Strideforth.

It was difficult to see their way. Glimmers of dim light filtered down from above. The walkway gave another lurch. Stella shot a glance back over her shoulder. The monster was close behind.

"Hurry!" she gasped.

They reached the end of the walkway and ran as fast as they could away from the pool, ducking between tanks and pipes and other obstacles. Stella's heart was hammering. A shape loomed up in front of her and she swerved around it. Somewhere in the darkness ahead, Henry shrieked.

Stella tripped over part of Jem's broken ladder and fell headlong into a puddle. She scrambled to her feet.

A deep cry echoed around the cavern.

It was the voice of the monster.

❧ Twenty-Three ❧

S tella stumbled on through the darkness. She heard a scuttling noise somewhere close by, and she jumped.

"Strideforth?" she called. Her voice was shaking. "Hortense? Jem?"

There was no answer. Her outstretched hands found the rough wall of the cavern, and she groped her way along it. The air was colder, and the clanks and hisses were getting fainter. Water trickled nearby.

The monster howled again.

Stella felt her legs trembling.

In *A Garden of Lilies*, Yaxley got lost in the dark. Stella could not remember exactly what happened to him, but it was something frightful. She tried not to think about it.

She imagined that Letty was beside her. Nothing

was as bad if there were two of you. She took a breath and made herself think about Wilberforce Montgomery, venturing boldly into caves and tunnels and all kinds of dangerous places, hunting out strange creatures for his collection. She went on with determination.

She heard voices ahead. A faint light flickered. Strideforth appeared, holding the stump of a candle. Stella gasped with relief.

"There you are," he said. "I was coming back for you. We have to stay together so nobody gets lost."

The candlelight showed a low, narrow tunnel with uneven rocky walls. Stella followed Strideforth, ducking her head. The stream trickled along beside them, disappearing into a rusty iron pipe.

"I had this candle and a matchbox in my pocket," Strideforth said. "But there was only one match left, and the candle is very short. It won't last long."

Around a bend in the tunnel, Hortense and Jem were waiting, huddled together. Hortense was holding Anya close to her chest and whispering to her. Henry was perched on her head, his feathers ruffled. He clicked his beak at Stella and frowned. Jem was wearing Strideforth's hairy coat. It was much too large for him. He was shivering and looked miserable.

"I'm that sorry I broke the lantern," he said.

Hortense patted his arm.

"It was an accident," said Strideforth.

The monster howled again. It was coming closer.

Strideforth looked back down the tunnel toward the cavern. "It's following us. We can't go back. We have to keep moving."

Jem said, "This is the way I came. Through the caves. We'll come out in the wood."

"Here, you go first." Strideforth passed the candle to Jem.

Jem looked doubtful but nodded, took the candle, and led the way. The tunnel was narrow and winding, following the course of the trickling stream. They clambered over rocks and squeezed through crevices and waded through the icy water. Fantastical shapes loomed around them; rock formations towered like hunched figures or speared down from the darkness overhead, like the fangs of enormous creatures.

The monster's voice echoed through the tunnels, rumbling like thunder.

They went on, passing through a large cavern, threading their way between curved, jagged rocks that looked like the rib bones of a whale. The candle sputtered, and all around, the shadows lurched and flickered.

Something glimmered in Stella's memory: hurrying through a cave by the light of a lantern.

Her mother held her by the hand, pulling her along. She cried and her mother comforted her. They had to go quickly and be very quiet.

Suddenly the candle hissed and went out.

"Ouch," said Jem. "It's burned down."

"We'll have to go on without it," said Strideforth.

Hortense's cold hand found Stella's in the darkness. Stella gave it a squeeze.

"We'll be all right," she said.

They went on as quickly as they could, feeling their way, hands outstretched, stumbling over rocks and crawling along narrow tunnels.

The darkness seemed to go on forever. Somewhere behind them, the monster howled.

At last Stella realized she could see vague shapes ahead. She heard the sound of cascading water. Around a bend, they came to the foot of a waterfall. It gleamed in the dim, misty light, plunging over mossy rocks and ferns, filling the air with icy spray.

"Come on," said Strideforth. He peered up the steep sides of the waterfall. "This is the way out." He clambered onto a wet rock and dragged Jem up beside him. Hortense climbed quickly. Stella scrambled up after them. She tried to grip with her fingers, but the rocks were slippery with moss and slime. Water splashed down around her. She coughed and wiped her wet hair out of her eyes. Strideforth leaned down, grabbed her hand, and pulled her up. "Keep going," he said. "You're nearly there."

Stella climbed as well as she could. Strideforth hauled her up over the last few rocks. She crawled out and sank down onto the ground, gasping. She was shaking and wet through. She took a deep breath and rolled over onto her back. Huge trees surrounded them, their branches reaching up into the sky. Her eyes were so used to the darkness of the caves that the stars seemed to glow as brightly as lamps in the mist, and the crescent moon made her blink.

She took another breath, sat up, and looked around. They had come out into a little clearing in the wood. The stream trickled out from between the trees and then dived into a hole, tumbling and splashing over the rocks before disappearing underground.

Strideforth leaned out precariously over the edge and looked down at the waterfall. "Is this where you fell, Jem?"

Jem nodded. "I think so. But I was running that fast, I din't stop and look."

A distant howl echoed up from deep below.

Strideforth backed away from the hole. He

grabbed Stella's hand and pulled her to her feet. "Come on," he said. "Let's go."

They made their way across the clearing toward the trees.

There was a sudden sharp whistle. Henry shrieked. A light glimmered. Dark figures appeared from the shadows.

Stella yelled in fright.

A strong hand gripped her arm. "Hold hard, cully."

❧ Twenty-Four ☙

Stella gasped, blinking. The lantern light glistened on the tarnished sequins of Mr. Flint's coat and on the teeth around his hatband. He put his fingers to his mouth and gave another sharp whistle.

Three young men, gap-toothed and vacant-looking, slouched into the light, dragging Strideforth, Hortense, and Jem. Strideforth was struggling and trying to yell, but the first man's hand was clamped tightly over his mouth. The second man held both Jem and Hortense, twisting their arms behind their backs. Jem was pale. Blood trickled from his nose. Hortense was wriggling and squeaking and trying to kick. The third youth gripped Anya by the scruff of her neck and had Henry clamped under his arm. Anya was making shrill, angry squeals and scratching and biting. Henry was shrieking and snapping his beak at his captor's face.

Mr. Flint said, "Get that rope from the wagon, boys. Put the little white whitterick in a cage. I'll see to it later. Shove that bleedin' bird in too, whatever it is. Quick, now."

The young man holding Anya and Henry gave him a nod and hurried off.

"Tie them nippers to the tree there." Mr. Flint pointed to a huge tree at the edge of the clearing. "Nice and tight, mind. Watch that hole, and fetch me when the monster turns up." He gripped Stella's arm. She tried to wrench herself away, but his fingers were like iron. "You're coming with me, cully," he said, and dragged her away into the trees.

"Let go," she gasped. She twisted around, trying to kick him. "What do you want? Let me go!"

He pulled her along, ignoring her struggles. They came out onto a winding, overgrown cart track. The dentist's wagon stood nearby, the horses resting between the shafts. There were squeaks and shrieks from inside. The young man jumped down, carrying a coil of rope. He looked rather badly bitten. He slouched off and disappeared into the trees.

Mr. Flint dragged Stella up the stairs, pushed her inside, and shut the door behind them.

The wagon was crammed so full of boxes and bundles stacked in untidy piles that there was only a small space to stand. Anya and Henry were in a small wire cage along with the two-headed chicken, balanced on top of a bundle of canvas. Henry shrieked and tried to flap his wings. Anya dashed from side to side, uttering piercing squeaks. The two-headed chicken crouched in the corner of the cage. It shivered and blinked, and each head gave a sad little cluck. Rows of jars and tins lined the walls of the wagon. Florence Nightingale, Dr. Livingstone, and the Duke of Wellington leaned together in a corner, their glass eyes glittering.

Mr. Flint hung the lantern on a hook overhead. "I had to strike the tent and move out, what with them coppers swarming all over the village," he said. "So I came here, quiet-like, to have a go at snabbling this monster. I don't like all these bleedin' trees, though. They make me uneasy, I don't mind telling you, cully. Give me a nice town street, gaslight, and hot oysters any day. We came past the crossroads back there"—he jerked a thumb over his shoulder— "and I saw something pale, flittin' along. Singing. My word on it. It gave me the frights, it did. And my lads, too. We come along past, lickety-split, then heard the monster bellowing, down there underground. So we hopped down from the wagon to take a gander. And here you come, waltzing up out of the hole, right into my hands. Just like that." He snapped his fingers and smiled.

"Wh-what do you want with me?"

Mr. Flint gestured at the rows of jam jars and soup tins. Stella saw that they were piled full of teeth. Hundreds and hundreds of gleaming teeth. Mr. Flint dipped his fingers into a jar, selected one, and held it up to show her. "Ever given much thought to your pie grinders, cully?" He looked at Stella with his head on the side, his green eyes glinting. "Full of secrets, teeth are. When I pull a tooth, I take a listen." He pushed the tooth into his ear. "Most people don't hear nothing. But me, I hear whispers. Things people don't like to talk about. Nasty little things sometimes, my dear young lady. My word on it. Shameful things. Dreadful stories such as might make your hair curl." He smiled. "All sorts." He took the tooth out of his ear and dropped it back into the jar with a clink.

"What do you mean?"

"Everything has a price, cully." He waved his hand around the wagon. "A two-headed chicken. A little white whitterick." He nodded at Anya, who hissed at him from between the bars of the cage, her fur bristling. "Even a stone what looks just like a toad. Curiosities. Sixpence here. A shilling there. But I've always got my lugs out for something special. I was over Brockley way and I heard whispers about this here monster. 'There's money in that, Jethro Flint,' I thought to myself. Shoved in a cage for people to gawp at. Or stuffed and mounted. Either way. 'The Wormwood Monster. Dead or Alive' (depending). 'Marvel of Nature.' Tickets only half a crown." He smiled again. "So I came here to get my grabblers on it. And while I'm here, I pull a few more teeth, and I hear a few more secrets, village gossip and tittle-tat, nothing out of the way. But then I pull an old woman's snaggler, and in that tooth I hear something special. A story about two nippers, ten years back. Strange little things, seeming. Fading in and out, like. Vanishing and appearing again. Uncanny, that."

"Fading? What—what do you mean?" Stella's voice shook.

"The family were rich coves, and they kept the strange little nippers tucked away, all alone with their ma, in a big house with a high wall all around.

The gate locked tight, and nobody allowed in or out. Keeping them secret, so nobody would find out what they was. And no wonder, neither. Rich coves don't like folk knowing there's something rum in their family tree. But the nippers went missing. One was gone for good, but the other one was found, so the story goes, right here in the wood, wandering all by herself. And now here she is. Back again." He grabbed Stella's arm once more and pulled her closer. "I've been keeping a close eye on you, cully. And I saw what you did, in the village. I saw you appear, right out of nothing." He nodded. "A monster is special, right enough. But a little mort what can fade herself away? That's singular, that is. That's bleedin' unique."

"N-no," Stella stammered.

Mr. Flint nodded again. "Yes, indeed. Everything has a price, my dear young lady. And there's ready money for a singular item like yourself. Ready money. My word on it."

❦❧ Twenty-Five ❦❧

Stella yelled and struggled. Mr. Flint's fingers bit into her arm.

"Yawl all you like, cully. Your little mates won't be coming to save you. My boys will see to that." He picked up a long pair of pliers from a shelf. "Now. How are your teeth? Any little niggles at all?" He snapped the jaws of the pliers. *Click, click.*

Stella tried to wrench herself out of his grasp.

"A little snick. Quick as a wink. You won't even know it's gone. I'll just pull two or three and have a listen. And after that, you'll be a sight more obliging, cully. Because when I've got ahold of a few of your secrets, I've got ahold of you. My three lads out there, I snabbled most of their teeth, and I keep them on my hat, and here on my ticker slang." He indicated the watch chain that hung across his waistcoat. A row of teeth dangled from it, like ivory fobs. "I left them enough for chewing their porridge." He laughed. "They don't think for themselves, overly much. Not anymore. But they do what I say. And you will too, my dear young lady."

Stella tried to pull away. She collided with the cage, making it rock. Anya squeaked and Henry shrieked.

"Open up," said Mr. Flint. *Click, click.* He dragged her closer.

Stella felt the cold metal of the pliers against her cheek. She twisted her head aside.

For some reason, the final story from *A Garden of Lilies* came into her mind. Zenobia answered back to her governess and was immediately sucked into a waterspout and whirled away.

> *Disaster comes to every child,*
> *Headstrong, willful, rude or wild.*

Stella groaned in exasperation. *A Garden of Lilies* was the most discouraging, unhelpful book ever written. That was certain. Right now, she had to be headstrong. She had to do something to escape and to rescue the others. With determination, she snaked her free hand behind her back and fumbled for the little piece of wire that held the door of the cage closed. She untwisted it and yanked open the door.

Anya and Henry shot out. Henry flew around the wagon, shrieking. Anya sank her teeth into Mr. Flint's nose and darted away. He yelled, let go of Stella's arm, and clutched his face. Henry landed on his head. "*Heus!*" he screeched. Mr. Flint thrashed his arms about. Henry kicked off his hat, snatched a tuft of his hair, and tried to pull it out. Mr. Flint shouted and staggered around the wagon. Henry flapped his wings and screamed.

Florence Nightingale, Dr. Livingstone, and the Duke of Wellington toppled over, knocking several boxes to the floor. The cage crashed down, and the two-headed chicken scuttled out and disappeared into a dark corner. Jars smashed and teeth scattered. Anya dashed in circles, leaping from box to box around the wagon, then onto Mr. Flint's face. She bit his nose again. He howled in pain.

The door opened. One of the young men stood on the step and stared vacantly at the chaos inside, his mouth hanging open. He made a gesture over his shoulder. "Monster's comin,'" he said.

Stella dived under Mr. Flint's

clutching fingers, swerved around the young man, jumped down the steps, and sprinted away into the trees. Henry flew after her, shrieking with excitement. Anya darted past her like a streak of light. Stella fled, bounding over roots, pushing through banks of ferns, ducking under overhanging branches. She could hear Mr. Flint close behind, crashing and cursing.

She came to the small clearing by the waterfall. Strideforth, Jem, and Hortense were sitting in a row, tied with rope to the trunk of the huge tree, their hands behind them. Strideforth had a bruise on his cheek. Jem's eyes were closed. Hortense was frowning as if she were trying not to cry.

Mr. Flint's other two men spun around when Anya and Henry burst into the clearing. Anya leaped onto Hortense's shoulder, chittering and squeaking, then darted away from her, dashed up the leg of one of the men, and bit him hard on the ear. He yelled. Henry swooped down at them, shrieking. The men covered their heads with their hands and stumbled around.

Stella ran over to the tree. "Are you all right?" she panted. She crouched and tried to untie the knots, but they were too tight.

"Grab my knife," said Strideforth. He wriggled around so she could reach his pocket. She fished out the pocketknife, opened a blade, and began to saw through the rope.

"Hurry!" Strideforth gasped.

Stella shot a glance behind. Mr. Flint appeared at the edge of the clearing. His hat was gone and his nose was bleeding. The third young man followed him, carrying the empty cage.

Stella kept hacking through the rope.

"Drop the knife, cully," said Mr. Flint. He strode over to grab her. She jumped up and turned to run, but tripped over a tree root and fell. The knife spun out of her hand. Before she could scramble to her feet again, Mr. Flint seized her arm.

Stella struggled and wrenched herself free. She backed away from him, took a breath, and forced herself to fade. Her head swam. She felt the horrible, dizzying sensation as she made herself disappear into the shadows.

Mr. Flint's fingers passed right through her.

Strideforth and the others gasped.

"Where are you? shouted Mr. Flint, spinning around.

Invisible, Stella held her breath and watched as he clutched at empty air.

Strideforth had pulled his arms free and untangled himself from the rope. He staggered upright and dragged Hortense and Jem to their feet. They turned to run, but before they could escape, Mr. Flint whirled around and seized Hortense by her neck. He held the pliers against her throat. She gave a choking scream.

"No!" yelled Strideforth. He hurled himself at Mr. Flint. One of the young men caught him and shoved him roughly to the ground. Henry swooped, snapping his beak. Anya darted up Mr. Flint's leg, squeaking.

"Snabble them bleedin' animals!" shouted Mr. Flint. "Shove 'em in that cage."

Jem sidled around behind Mr. Flint and lunged toward him, but he was caught and hurled aside.

One of the men snatched up Anya by the scruff of her neck. She squeaked and wriggled and hissed as he pushed her into the cage. Another grabbed Henry, jammed him in, shrieking and snapping, and slammed the door.

Mr. Flint dragged Hortense toward the waterfall.

Strideforth struggled upright, but his leg gave way under him and he fell. "Leave her alone," he gasped.

Mr. Flint ignored him. He called out, "All right, then, my dear young lady. I know you're here. So show yourself, nice and quiet, and your mates will go free. Otherwise, I'll toss them down the hole to the bleedin' monster. One by one. This little mort's goin' first."

"No!" yelled Strideforth.

Henry shrieked. Anya squeaked and hissed and spat.

Mr. Flint held Hortense over the edge of the waterfall. She was shaking, and her face was pale. "I'll count to three," he said, smiling. "And down she goes. One—"

Stella forced herself to appear again, as quickly as she could. She felt dizzy and sick. The wood seemed to be tilting from side to side. She took a faltering step forward. "Here I am."

Mr. Flint flung Hortense aside. He strode across and grabbed Stella by the wrist, twisting her arm behind her back. She gasped in pain.

Strideforth and Jem scrambled toward Hortense and helped her to her feet.

Mr. Flint smiled grimly. "Tie 'em up again, lads. Good and tight, this time."

"You said you'd let them go," said Stella.

"You be quiet, or I'll knock 'em on the head and toss 'em down that hole. After we're gone, someone will happen along this way and find 'em, like enough." Mr. Flint gave Stella's arm a vicious wrench. She cried out as pain shot through her wrist.

"Stella!" said Strideforth.

Suddenly the monster howled. Loud and close.

"It's comin' up," called one of the young men, peering down into the hole. He backed away quickly.

The ferns at the edge of the waterfall moved. Then the monster's head appeared. It hesitated, its tiny eyes glinting in the lantern light, then it slithered up out of the hole and into the clearing. It was enormous. Almost as long as a train carriage and as wide as a wine barrel. Moonlight shone on its leathery black skin.

Mr. Flint gasped. "Look at the size of it. Stuffed and mounted, it'll be worth a bleedin' fortune. Forget them nippers, lads. Grab that rope and snabble it."

The monster's black tongue flicked in and out as if it were tasting the air. It opened its mouth, revealing rows of glittering, silvery teeth, and howled.

The young men reluctantly made their way toward it, uncoiling the rope as they went. One made a nervous, halfhearted grab at it. The monster twisted around, snapping. The young man jumped back.

"Sapskulls. Get that rope around it!" yelled Mr. Flint. He backed away, dragging Stella with him. Stella struggled, but he was twisting her arm so hard, she thought she might faint.

The young men approached the monster again.

It lashed its tail from side to side.

Out of the corner of her eye, Stella saw Strideforth limping around the edge of the clearing. He dashed out of the trees and flung himself onto Mr. Flint from behind. He clung on, his arms locked around the dentist's neck. Mr. Flint yelled and reeled about.

Jem and Hortense tried to pull Stella away. Mr. Flint lost his balance and fell. He hit the ground with a heavy thump. Stella rolled away from him and scrambled to her feet.

The monster turned in a flash and slithered toward them.

Hortense screamed.

"Run!" shouted Jem.

Stella grabbed his arm before he could move. "No! No!" she gasped. "No! Don't run. Stay still."

She gripped Jem's arm and held her breath. She could feel him trembling and hear her own heart beating in her ears. Every particle in her body wanted to flee. Strideforth was pale, holding Hortense's hand tight. Her eyes were wide with fear.

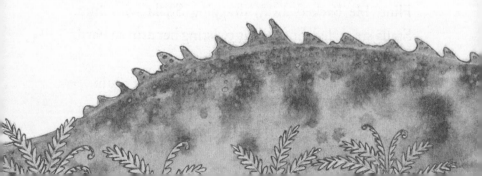

The monster's black tongue flickered in and out again. The young men shrank back uneasily.

"Stay still," whispered Stella.

The monster passed between them all, close enough to touch. Stella could smell its breath, sharp and salty, and see tiny beads of water glistening on its back.

Mr. Flint was gasping and gibbering with panic. He crawled away from the monster, staggered to his feet, and turned to run.

Like lightning, the monster lunged and struck. Its teeth sank into Mr. Flint's leg.

He fell down. Screaming, he pulled himself along the ground, lurched upright, and staggered into the middle of the clearing. Gasping for breath, he took a stiff step backward, and then another one. He teetered on the edge of the waterfall, clutching at the air.

There was a sharp cracking sound.

They watched, horrified, as he turned to stone. His whole body stiffened. His skin became a dull gray. For a second he hung there, back arched, stone

eyes staring blindly up at the night sky, stone hands reaching into the cold air. Then he toppled backward and disappeared from sight, crashing onto the rocks below.

The monster roared. It turned its head toward the hole, tongue flickering in and out. Then it slithered back to the waterfall, slid over the edge, and plunged down into the darkness.

After a moment, from deep underground, it howled again.

Stella took a breath, and then another one. She tiptoed nervously toward the hole and looked down. The monster was gone. At the bottom of the waterfall lay the stone statue that had been Mr. Flint. A collection of shattered rocks and crumpled clothes. The sequined coat was wet in the spray from the waterfall. A broken stone hand with curled fingers was still clutching at the air.

Mr. Flint's young men leaned over and stared blankly down.

The first one wiped his mouth and said, "Will you look at that?"

"I'm right clemmed, I am," commented the second young man.

"I could drink a pint of stingo," remarked the third one. He ran his tongue over his gums. He looked around, bewildered. "What are all them nippers doing here?" Without waiting for an answer, he turned and drifted away toward the cart track. The other two hesitated for a moment, confused. One of them opened his mouth to say something, but then shut it again. They wandered off in the same direction, disappearing amongst the trees.

Jem came over and looked down the hole. "Coo," he said.

Hortense opened the cage and took Henry and Anya into her arms, stroking them and whispering to them.

"Are you all right?" Strideforth asked Stella.

She nodded and rubbed her bruised wrist. "Are you?"

"Yes." He grinned.

Hortense turned to Stella. She opened her mouth and croaked, in a hoarse, unfamiliar voice, "Thank you."

Stella took her hand and squeezed it. "Thank you, too," she said.

Strideforth laughed. He gave Hortense a hug that lifted her off the ground. "Now we can go home," he said.

Twenty-Six

They walked together through the trees toward the cart track.

Stella was shivering with cold. She felt battered, and her wrist was aching and bruised. She thought about Mr. Flint. It had been horrifying to see him bitten by the monster and then turn into stone and fall down the waterfall, crashing into pieces. He had been very bad. And he had come to a dreadful end.

A small creature scuttled into the ferns. Hortense darted after it. She came back, cradling the two-headed chicken in her arms. She stroked it and made crooning sounds. Both of the chicken's heads clucked to her. Anya chittered at it, and Henry snapped his beak.

As they approached the cart track, they heard the sounds of horses' hooves and harnesses jingling.

The dentist's wagon rolled toward them. The three young men were sitting up on the box. One of them held the reins, and the other two were passing a bottle back and forth. Strideforth stumbled out onto the track, shouting and waving his arms, but they ignored him, and the wagon lurched past and disappeared into the night.

"Well, we can walk," Strideforth said with a shrug.

They followed the track as it wound through the dark wood. Misty moonlight shone through the branches of the trees, making the twigs and moss and all the little curling ferns gleam like silver. The stars sparkled overhead. Somewhere in the darkness, an owl hooted.

Strideforth grinned awkwardly at Stella. He said, "So, you know it is impossible for you to disappear like you did. That is certain."

Stella smiled back at him. "I know."

"How do you do it?"

"I don't know. It used to just happen sometimes, when I was trying to hide. Now I can make it happen. Mr. Flint said my sister was the same. When we were little, we used to fade away and vanish, he said."

"How did he know about you?"

"He could hear people's secrets in their teeth. He heard about me in Mrs. Burdock's tooth."

"That is also impossible," commented Strideforth.

"Yes," agreed Stella. "But that was the secret she was keeping. And he saw me disappear, in the village. He wanted to put me on show in his tent, I think. Or maybe sell me to someone." She shuddered.

"It's a very strange thing to be able to do," said Strideforth. "To disappear like that."

Stella nodded. "Yes. My mother came to stay at Wormwood Mire when we were babies so nobody would find out about us. My Aunts sent her away, I think. They wouldn't have liked strange disappearing babies at all. They disapprove of everything. They wanted to keep us secret. My mother found the way out, through the caves. She got that message. I think she tried to escape and meet someone."

"What happened to her?" asked Strideforth.

Stella said, "I don't know." She thought about the monster. Had it bitten her mother, just as it had bitten Mr. Flint? That was a horrible idea.

They walked on in silence for several minutes.

As if he had been thinking the same thing, Strideforth

said, "We'll have to let the furnace go cold. And then the monster will go back to sleep, do you think?"

Stella nodded. "I hope so."

The track turned and began to slope downward. Huge gnarled trees crowded together. Tendrils of mist curled and drifted in the faint glimmers of moonlight that filtered down through the tangled branches overhead.

They passed piles of enormous mossy stones. "The giants' castle," whispered Jem. "From the old days."

"There's no such thing as giants," said Strideforth, but he sounded uncertain as he looked nervously around at the looming, shadowy stones.

They came to a crossroads. In the middle was an ancient stone marker.

Stella stopped. She remembered the little note in the musical box: *Crossroads. Midnight. I will wait.*

Strideforth hesitated. "We have to keep going."

And then, drifting through the night, they heard a distant, whispering voice.

Someone was singing.

Jem gasped, his face white. "The ghost," he said softly. "It's the singing girl." He stumbled backward, falling over his own feet. "Come on."

"Let's go," said Strideforth. He and Hortense turned and hurried after Jem.

Stella hardly noticed them leave. She stood and listened. The voice sang on, a whispering, melancholy tune, like raindrops falling on wet leaves. Stella's breath caught in her throat. She walked away from the track, in between the ancient trees. Her footsteps were silent on a carpet of moss and dead leaves. She passed beside stone walls, tangled with ivy, ducking through a shadowy opening that might have once been a doorway.

In a glade, a pale shape was singing, drifting from side to side like a wisp of smoke.

Stella stepped out from the shadows. The faint shape hesitated and then darted away. Stella took a shaky breath, unbuttoned her coat, and felt in the pocket of her dress for the musical box. She took out the key, wound it around, and opened the lid.

The tinkling tune floated through the dark trees.

There was a flicker at the edge of the glade. The pale shape drifted closer and began to sing along with the musical box. Its voice was no louder than a sigh. It sang on and on until the tinkling music slowed and stopped.

In the silence, Stella held out her hand.

The shape hovered for a moment. Then, like steam condensing on a cold window, it slowly formed itself into a thin girl with wide, startled eyes. Her mouse-colored hair straggled down over her shoulders. She wore a shapeless cotton dress. Her feet were bare.

Looking at her face was like looking into a mirror.

"Letty?" whispered Stella.

"I'm Luna," the girl said. She shot a glance over her shoulder. Tentatively, she put out her hand and touched Stella's. Her fingers were very cold.

"Luna." Stella felt a lump in her throat. "I'm Stella," she said. "I'm your sister." She swallowed. "I'm your sister," she repeated.

"Stella." Luna nodded. "I seen you. In the sweetshop. And then on the green. I followed you to the big house. She wanted me to put a thorn on you. But I wouldn't. So she did it herself."

"Who?"

"Gram. Mrs. Spindleweed."

"But why?"

"She wants you to go away. She's right fierce for secrets, she is. 'Stay secret, stay safe,' she says." Luna touched the musical box with her finger. "What's that?"

"It's a musical box. You were singing the same tune."

Luna said, "I always sing it to the gray lady. I sneak out at night. Gram don't know."

"Who is the gray lady?"

"She's a secret." Luna hesitated, then tugged Stella's

hand. "I found her, a long time ago. She's special. I'll show you. Come an' see."

She led Stella across the glade. A huge tree arched overhead. Luna ducked under a low branch and crept between the ruined stone walls, pulling Stella behind her.

They passed through shadow and came out again into moonlight. In a sheltered corner stood the mossy stone statue of a woman. Ivy tangled around her, like a gown of leaves. Her arms stretched out, as if in protection. Snowdrops and groundsel, winter flowers, were arranged in patterns around her feet. She wore a necklace of rosehips and acorns and twisted silvery sweets wrappers, and on her head was a crown of mistletoe.

"I always come and sing to her," said Luna. "An' I bring her flowers. But in the winter, there aren't many."

A beam of pale moonlight slanted down through the branches of the tree and shone on the statue. She looked fragile and sad. Her wide eyes were almost too large for her thin face. Stella tried to speak, but no words came out. She touched the statue's hand.

"She's special, ain't she?" said Luna.

Stella swallowed and whispered, "She's our mother."

"Mother?" Luna said the word as if she had never heard it before.

"Yes." A tear trickled down Stella's cheek. She showed Luna the lid of the musical box. "This was hers. Look. It says 'Patience.' That was our mother's name. She used to sing us this song. When we were little."

The silver letters gleamed dimly in the moonlight. Luna traced them with her finger, then the tiny silver moon and star. Stella opened the musical box and took out the photograph. She tilted it so that the beam of moonlight shone on it. "Can you see? That's me. That's you. Or maybe the other way round. I can't tell us apart. And that's our mother."

Luna touched the three faces one by one with the tip of her finger. She looked from the face of the woman in the photograph to the statue. She nodded.

"And look." Stella showed her the tiny piece of paper, although the moonlight was not bright enough to read the faint writing. "It says *Crossroads. Midnight. I will wait.* She escaped from Wormwood Mire and brought us here through the tunnels and caves. To meet someone at the crossroads."

"Who?" asked Luna.

"I don't know. I think it might have been our father."

"Our father," repeated Luna.

"I don't know who he was," said Stella. "I don't know anything about him. Perhaps he came and waited for her at the crossroads. But the monster must have followed her and chased her and bitten her. When they found she was gone from the house, they searched everywhere, but they never found her, and they never found you. They only found me."

"Gram found me in the wood. She heard me crying. I was all by myself. She din't see me, though, because I was faded. I din't know I had a mother. Or a father. Or a sister, neither."

"And I thought you were dead," said Stella.

"And now we found us ourselves," said Luna. She squeezed Stella's hand.

Stella showed her the little dolls. "Look. This one was yours. This one was mine."

Luna took her doll gently and stared at it in amazement. Her fingers curled around it. "Yes," she whispered.

Stella closed the musical box and pushed it into her pocket. She took a last look at her mother. She reached up and stroked her cold stone cheek. Then she clasped Luna's hand. Their fingers twined together, gripping tightly.

"Come with me. Come and meet our cousins," she said.

~ Twenty-Seven ~

They passed between the ruined stone walls, in and out of moonlight and shadow. As they reached the edge of the glade, an owl hooted nearby. Luna stiffened.

"It's her," she whispered. Her fingers tightened on Stella's hand.

"Who?"

"Gram."

A pale shape flew into the glade, landing on the low branch of a tree. A huge owl with round yellow eyes. "Hooo-hooo," it cried.

"It's her owl?" whispered Stella.

"No, it's *her*."

The owl swooped silently down to the ground. In an easy movement, like a cat waking up and stretching, it shifted and transformed. Where the owl had been, Mrs. Spindleweed now stood, glaring.

Stella gasped.

The old woman was wrapped in a black shawl embroidered with a pattern of feathers and stars. She gazed fiercely at Stella. "Who are you?" she asked. "Who?"

Luna took a step forward. "She's my sister. My sister, Stella."

Mrs. Spindleweed hissed. "I told you, Tick. Stay hid. And stay out of the wood." She fixed her yellow eyes on Stella. "And you, girl. You keep away."

"She's my sister, Gram," said Luna. "She's same as me."

Mrs. Spindleweed came closer to Stella and stared into her eyes. The old woman smelled of peppermint and licorice and something musty that Stella did not recognize. "Stop your poking and prying, girl. I'll make you sorry. It'll be worse than thorns next time."

"You leave her be," said Luna.

Mrs. Spindleweed glared. "It's for your own good, Tick. You don't know what the world is, but I do. It ain't safe for the likes of us. It ain't safe for anyone fey. There's danger everywhere. Stay secret, stay safe. There ain't no other way."

She turned to Stella. "There's danger for you, too, girl. And more danger still, for two of you together."

Stella thought about Mr. Flint and how he had tried to snatch her away. She knew what Mrs. Spindleweed said was true.

"I wasn't after hurting you, with them thorns," Mrs. Spindleweed said. "I was keeping you away. I was keeping Tick safe."

Stella gripped Luna's hand. "But we're sisters. We're the same."

"Two sides of a coin, you are," Mrs. Spindleweed agreed. "But you're sometimes faded, and Tick's sometimes seen. Two sides of a coin. Night and day. It happens that way, with twins." The old woman looked intently into Stella's eyes. "I keep Tick safe. Ever since I found her, all by herself, faded away and crying in the wood. I've kept her safe all this time." She beckoned to Luna. "And I will now. Come, Tick."

Stella took a breath. "Please, Mrs. Spindleweed," she said. "Please. Come and— I mean, I would like Luna to meet my cousins. Our cousins." She added, "And you too, of course."

Mrs. Spindleweed wrapped her shawl firmly around herself. "No," she said.

"Please, Gram," said Luna.

The old woman shook her head. "No. For what purpose? To bring trouble raining down on us? No."

"But—"

Voices were approaching through the trees. Mrs. Spindleweed darted a look over her shoulder. "Promise me you'll keep quiet, girl. Keep our secret." She fixed her yellow eyes on Stella once more. "Stay secret, stay safe. Promise me."

Stella nodded. Tears were pricking her eyes. "I promise."

"Tick," said Mrs. Spindleweed. She reached out her hand.

Luna made a choking sound. She gave Stella a quick, tight hug, and then stepped away. In the blink of an eye, she vanished.

Stella felt cold, invisible fingers touching hers. They gripped for a moment, and then let go. She was left holding empty air. "Luna!"

Mrs. Spindleweed's strange eyes were fierce and proud. "Good fortune, girl," she said to Stella.

In a swift, sure movement, she transformed into the enormous bird again. Stella caught a glimpse of Luna, a pale, wispy shape, climbing onto her back. The owl gave Stella one last yellow-eyed glare, stretched out its wings, and took flight, swooping through the trees.

Stella stood and gazed after it as it flew up into the starry sky.

The voices were coming closer. A dog barked. Lantern light flickered through the trees.

Strideforth appeared, ducking between the stones. "Stella!"

Hortense and Jem followed him, together with a group of men with lanterns and long sticks and several dogs. Mr. Burdock was beaming, his arm around Jem's shoulders.

"Stella! There you are," said Strideforth. "Here's the search party. They were looking for Jem."

Stella took a shaky breath and wiped the tears from her face.

"What happened?" asked Strideforth. "You're crying. Are you all right?"

"It was nothing," she said.

"We heard voices. I saw—"

"It was nothing," said Stella again. She took another breath. "It was just an owl." Something pale caught her eye. A little feather lay on the ground. She picked it up and ran her finger along it. Then she opened the musical box and put the feather beside the doll that lay there alone.

"It was just an owl," she repeated. And she closed the lid of the box with a snap.

⌒⟲⟳⌒

They followed the track through the trees to the edge of the wood and climbed the slope up to the bridge. As they reached the gates of Wormwood Mire, Mrs. Burdock rushed out of the gatehouse, shrieking. She wrapped Jem in a tight hug. She gave him a thump on the head and another hug. Then she hugged Mr. Burdock, some of the men from the search party, and then Jem again.

Miss Araminter patted Strideforth and Stella and Hortense. "There you are, my dears," she said, smiling. "Horehound and wormwood and Patagonian ginger root, for the cold." She looked down at Stella's bruised wrist. "And henbane and comfrey for you. I will make an infusion."

Mrs. Burdock clicked her tongue. "Come inside. There's hot soup."

She bustled them all into the gatehouse and hurried the children upstairs to her tiny bedroom. Miss Araminter helped them take off their wet clothes and wrap themselves in quilts and blankets. Mrs. Burdock bundled up their clothes and took them away, muttering busily to herself.

They washed some of the grime off their hands and faces. Henry poked around on Mrs. Burdock's dressing table, kicking several things onto the floor. Anya hissed at the two-headed chicken while Hortense clucked at it and patted it consolingly. Stella pulled Mrs. Burdock's horn-backed hairbrush through her hair. She noticed Hortense watching her.

"Would you like me to brush your hair?" Stella asked.

Hortense hesitated and then nodded. Her hair was like a bird's nest. Stella managed to remove most of the knots and tangles. She brushed it and plaited it, despite Anya's squeaks and angry nips. Strideforth cut a short length from the ball of twine in his pocket, and Stella bound it around the end of the plait. She stood back and rubbed her bitten fingers.

"Very neat," said Miss Araminter approvingly.

Strideforth said, "That's how Mother did your hair. You look just like you used to, Hortense."

Hortense looked in the mirror and gave herself a tiny smile.

Back downstairs, the men of the search party were crowded into the parlor, talking and laughing and drinking bowls of vegetable soup. Mrs. Burdock pushed the children into chairs beside the crackling fire and gave them soup and thick pieces of bread and butter.

The soup was hot and delicious. When they finished, Mrs. Burdock filled their bowls for a second time.

Hortense fed little pieces of bread and butter to Henry and Anya, and to both heads of the two-headed chicken.

"Oh! Before I forget. This came for you, last post yesterday." Mrs. Burdock took a letter from the mantelpiece and passed it to Strideforth.

The envelope had a row of colored stamps on it. "Father," gasped Strideforth. He put down his spoon and, with trembling fingers, opened the envelope and unfolded the letter. He read it through, and then turned to Hortense with a grin. "He's coming home. He's already on his way." Strideforth laughed. "He missed us, Hortense."

Hortense gave a sudden wide smile. "Good," she said.

Jem was finishing his third bowl of soup. His eyes were closing. He yawned.

"Bed for you," said Mrs. Burdock.

Miss Araminter stood up and said, "Yes, indeed. Thank you for the soup, Mrs. Burdock. Come, my dears."

Outside, the sun was rising. The sky was a pale gray, shiny and silvery like the inside of a seashell. Little birds twittered in the branches of the trees. Stella blinked and watched the hazy light turn the clouds yellow and orange and pink.

As she walked down the drive to Wormwood Mire, an image came into her head, almost like a dream. For a moment she was flying through the sky on the back of an owl. She could feel the soft feathers beneath her and the beating of silent wings. The icy air rushed past. She was part of the wind, and the morning light shone right through her.

Stella gazed up into the sunshine, feeling the cold breeze on her face.

She thought about Luna, her sister.

And she smiled.

Acknowledgments

I'd like to thank my sister Ruth and my brother-in-law Cesar for their support and for their excellent suggestions and ideas; Suzanne Willis for reading the manuscript and for her help and encouragement; Lu Sexton and Liz Self and everyone who has had to listen to all my writing problems; Ben Wood for the very useful Victorian dictionary; Chris Kunz; all the lovely people at ABC Books, especially Chren Byng, Kate Burnitt, Cristina Cappelluto, and Hazel Lam; everyone at Atheneum, especially Reka Simonsen; and my agent, Jill Corcoran.